PUMPKIN SPICE & PROPHECIES

A SMALL-TOWN HALLOWEEN ROMANTIC COMEDY

KAYE KENNEDY

DEDICATION

For anyone who has ever been made to feel like they had to self-abandon to earn love

NOTE FROM THE AUTHOR

Hi, Spooky Friends!

I can't thank you enough for choosing to read Shaunie & Harrison's love story. If this is the first of my books you've picked up, welcome! I typically write dramatic full-length novels featuring everyday heroes in uniform set in a big city, so this small-town romantic comedy is a bit different, but hopefully you will want to check out my first responder world, too.

Halloween is my birthday, so of course it's my favorite holiday. I love everything about the fall: the fashion, the flavors, the foliage, (the frights, not so much). This book is my love letter to autumn. I'm about to make a bold statement... Shaunie is my favorite heroine I have written thus far. Unintentionally, I put a lot more of myself into her than I'd intended, but I couldn't have hoped for a better outcome. She's the personification of chaos wrapped in pumpkin spice, and I feel that!

The other element I've infused into this book from my life is the psychic medium plot line because in addition to being an author, I am also a psychic medium. So this book is truly a marriage of my favorite things: pumpkin spice and prophecies.

This book is the first I have written after a long break from publishing. It felt good to get behind a keyboard again, but more than that, it was magical to see how far my writing has come since my baby author years. Hopefully, you appreciate my evolution, too.

If you're reading this around Halloween, I wish you and your family a safe spooky season filled with apple cider donuts, leaf piles, and pumpkin patches. If you're reading this during a different time of the year, I hope the message of owning who you are resonates, because it certainly doesn't have to be a ghoulish holiday for us to be reminded of who we are beneath our masks.

I hope you enjoy reading this as much as I enjoyed writing it!

Hugs & Happily Ever Afters,

Kaye Kennedy

ONE

"Okay, tell me you've heard about this. Annabelle—yes, *that* Annabelle, the demon doll that's basically the Beyoncé of haunted objects—has a new daddy." I grinned at my microphone, proud of that line.

The sound studio around us hummed with its usual mix of energy and claustrophobia. The faint ozone smell from the overworked soundboard filled the air, fighting for dominance against the lingering bitterness of my co-host's coffee. Harrison drank it black—gross! I'm a PSL kind of lady (that's pumpkin spice latte). I drink them year-round because...yum.

"You'll never guess who it is." I leaned into the mic and locked eyes with Harrison who looked like he regretted his life choices right about then. You see, he was originally my audio engineer, but while we were filming an early episode of *The Unexplained Files*, the jerk jumped in and argued with me about whether the St. Augustine lighthouse in Florida was haunted. (Are you freaking kidding me?! Like that's even debatable!) I saw the ghosts of the two little girls who'd died there in the late 1800s with my own eyes when

I'd visited a couple of years ago. The trip was part of my YouTube vlog, which had landed me this podcast gig. Anyway, my producer, Marty, ate up our banter, and that's how Harrison the Sound Guy became Harrison, my co-host.

We're total opposites, which somehow makes for an entertaining podcast. My side of the desk was scattered chaos—colorful pens, a chipped pumpkin-shaped mug painted with a sugar skull design, a notepad filled with doodles. Harrison's side, of course, looked like it had been curated for an IKEA ad. Notes stacked perfectly. Pens aligned in military formation. His laptop angled at a perfect ninety degrees to the mic.

"Are you gonna guess?" I prompted.

He scratched at the stubble that permanently covered his chin. The man could best be described as a hot nerd, although I'd never say that to him—the hot part, that is. The nerd side was undeniable. At thirty years old, he wore vintage cartoon tees under his flannels on the regular (calling them vintage is me being nice because he has probably had them since high school). Still, he had no idea that he was sneaky hot with his defined biceps and curly dark hair that was long-ish on top and short on the sides. It was the kind of style that made you want to thread your fingers through it and tug. Well, not me, of course, but some other girls, definitely.

"Snoop Dogg," he finally replied.

"If Snoop Dogg owned Annabelle, he would drop it like it's hot." I placed a hand over my diaphragm and let out an unfiltered laugh.

Harrison rolled his eyes so dramatically I thought they were going to tumble right out of his sockets.

"See what I did there?" I winked. Sometimes, I felt like I was talking to myself.

The insulated panels on the walls swallowed up any outside noise, making the room feel like we were sealed in a padded coffin. Wires coiled lazily across the floor, and the red *ON AIR* light glared down at us from its perch above the glass booth window, judging me every time I spiraled into tangent territory... which was often. Better to overfill silence than risk it swallowing me whole. Thankfully, we pre-recorded our episodes, so parts could be edited out if I went too far off topic.

"Hilarious," he replied dryly. "Snoop has his hands in many ventures. Why not a demon doll?"

I fiddled with the trio of rings stacked on my pointer finger as I considered his point. I'd gotten the fidget rings to help with my anxiety and such. Can't say whether or not they worked, but they were fun to play with. "Okay, maybe that's not such a bad guess. Did you know he has children's songs? There's a whole series on YouTube. Animated dogs who sing and rap nursery rhymes and stuff." I didn't have kids, but my channel had a quarter-million subscribers, so I kept my finger on the pulse of what happened on the platform as a whole.

"Interesting," Harrison said, not sounding the least bit amused, before guiding me back on track. "So, who owns this doll now?"

"Wait for it..." My brows danced.

"That's what we've been doing, Shaunie." He drew circles with his finger to hurry me along.

"Right...comedian Matt Rife—yes, that Matt Rife—just bought the Warrens' Occult Museum in Monroe, Connecticut, which is just a few hours south of where we're located in Boston, and where Annabelle has been locked up for decades, save for when she's on tour, obvi. And do you know what he's turning it into?" I couldn't wait for him to respond. "An Airbnb."

I slapped my palm on the desk for emphasis, making the bangles on my wrist jingle. *Oops.* That would have to be edited out in post. "An Airbnb, Harrison! Who in their right mind thinks: *Sure, let's spend the night with the most cursed Raggedy Ann doll in history. What could possibly go wrong?*"

"Tourists," Harrison said flatly, not even glancing up from his notes. His voice had that maddeningly calm baritone, like a parent indulging a child who had eaten too much sugar. "It's called capitalism, Shaunie. People want a thrill, and Matt Rife and his business partner..." He scrolled down his iPad with clinical precision, "...YouTuber Elton Castee, want money. Everybody wins."

I gasped, hand flying to my chest. "Everybody *dies*, you mean. Have you heard the stories? People who taunted Annabelle? Dead. Motorcycle crash. Heart attack. You name it. If ghosts don't get you, the karma will."

He finally lifted his gaze above the rim of his glasses, his brown eyes unreadable behind the faint glare of the studio lights. "Correlation isn't causation. People die every day. Even those who've never once met a doll."

I leaned closer to the mic, lowering my voice like I was telling a campfire story. "Do you even know how many people have died after provoking Annabelle? A priest who tried to exorcise her? Dead in a car crash. A guy who mocked her at the museum? Dead on his motorcycle before he even made it home. And don't get me started on the guy who tapped her case and laughed. Heart attack. Right there in the parking lot."

"Or," Harrison drawled, "humans being fragile meat-suits who sometimes crash their cars, sometimes have bad hearts, and sometimes do stupid things on motorcycles. News at eleven."

"Fragile meat-suits?" I feigned offense. "Listen to you, turning us into biology. You're such a robot. Admit it, if Annabelle winked at you, you'd scream like a toddler in Spirit Halloween."

Marty leaned into his mic on the other side of the glass and his muffled laugh buzzed into our headphones, "For the record, I'd pay to see that."

Harrison's jaw ticked, but his eyes cut up at Marty like he was personally betrayed. "You're supposed to be impartial."

"Hey, I produce podcasts, not referee hockey games," Marty shot back. He grinned, lifting his oversized mug. Today's said *Podcast Dad* in peeling block letters. I'd gifted him that one because he wrangled us like a father with toddlers. His desk was a shrine to mugs. *World's Okayest Producer. You're On Mute. Coffee Before Talkee.* The man collected ceramic red flags, and I adored him for it.

"Ugh, you're impossible." I leaned back in my chair and dramatically tossed my wavy, pink-tipped blond hair over my shoulder. The studio chair creaked, threatening to pitch me backward if I got too enthusiastic—again. "Fine. But when Annabelle shows up in your room at three a.m., don't expect me to save you."

"Statistically speaking, I'll be fine. But thanks for the concern." His lips twitched in that almost-smile that was basically a shout of emotion by Harrison's standards.

I narrowed my eyes at him, though it only made his smirk widen. "One day your statistics are gonna fail you, and I'm not giving the eulogy at your funeral."

"Because you'll be too busy making it about yourself?"

I slapped the table again, bracelets clattering. "Excuse me, I give excellent eulogies. People cry. They laugh. They leave feeling alive." I clutched my chest. "Honestly, it's a public service."

"Uh-huh." He glanced at the clock on the studio wall. "We're almost out of time."

"Fine, fine." I straightened and leaned into the mic, dialing back into podcast-host mode. "That's all for this week's *Unexplained Files*, but don't worry, next episode is going to be *huge*. We're hitting the road for a special Halloween series." I wiggled my fingers toward the glass, and Marty gave me a thumbs up. "That's right. We'll be recording on location in Sage Hollow, New Hampshire, a town famous for two things: its annual fall festival and Esme, the Medium Matchmaker."

"Reputable source, I'm sure," Harrison muttered.

Ignoring him, I turned my brightest grin toward the mic even though our listeners would only hear it. "Esme has promised us an exclusive interview, and who knows? Maybe she'll even help me find my soulmate."

"Shaunie…" Harrison's warning tone came too late.

Once the floodgate opened, I was sliding into tangent territory. "Look, dating apps are a nightmare. Swipe left, swipe right, swipe until your thumb cramps, and all you get is guys who open with 'hey beautiful' like they're allergic to originality. Or worse, the ones who think holding a fish in their profile picture is a personality trait. I mean, what am I supposed to do with that? Get excited about starting a seafood restaurant together?"

Behind the glass, Marty was doubled over, shoulders shaking with laughter.

"Is a man who can provide food for his family really so bad?" Harrison quipped.

"You're missing the point. And you can't judge because you don't date. We're on our second season of this show and not once have I heard you talk about a girl. Have you ever even been on a dating app?"

He crossed his arms over his chest, which was adorned with a *Teenage Mutant Ninja Turtles* tee. "I date."

I let out an exaggerated gasp. "You've heard it here first, folks. Harrison Moretti is *not* a thirty-year-old virgin."

He turned toward the glass. "Edit that out."

"Aww, don't be such a spoilsport, Harry," I teased. He hated when I called him that, which of course, made it more fun for me.

As per usual, his jaw ticked. "Focus." Harrison's voice had that tight edge he used when reeling me back in without making me sound completely unhinged. It always gave me a second to catch up to my mouth. Annoying. Helpful. Both.

Damn ADHD. I blew out a sigh. "Fine. Sage Hollow. Halloween. Ghosts, mediums, maybe love. You're not gonna wanna miss it."

Harrison leaned into his mic for the sign-off. "Or, if you'd like to hear an actual investigation grounded in logic and research rather than Shaunie's ongoing dating crises, we'll be bringing you that too."

I stuck my tongue out at him as the red recording light flicked off.

"Solid show," Marty said as he pushed through the door, grinning.

Our producer-slash-referee, looked like he hadn't seen the sun in weeks. His black-rimmed glasses were perpetually smudged, and his mop of graying hair needed taming, but he had quick wit and a quicker laugh. His sneakers squeaked as he crossed the studio floor, coffee mug in hand.

He dropped a printout of the tentative Sage Hollow schedule on our desk. "Check it. I got Esme for Tuesday, festival permit for street recording on Wednesday, and a tour slot at the Inn. Local council is thrilled. Or terrified. Hard to tell in an email."

"Thrilled," I decided. "They heard about my divination skills."

"Terrified. They heard about your decibel level," Harrison muttered as he took the printout and scanned it like we were prepping for a rocket launch.

"Two rooms?" I asked Marty as I stood and circled the desk so I could peer over Harrison's shoulder.

"Obviously," my co-host said, too quickly, and then seeming to realize how that sounded, color crept up his neck. "I mean—logistics."

Marty smirked. "Relax. The Inn's old. We're lucky it has more than one outlet per room."

I scribbled on my notepad: *bring extension cord, pumpkin socks, sexy witch PJs (j/k...maybe), cinnamon brooms, snacks (Twizzlers)*. I tapped my pen against the page, then added *Winnie's backpack carrier* because I wasn't leaving town without my cat. She went everywhere with me. Presently, she was napping in her bed just outside the sound booth.

"What do you need from us?" Harrison asked Marty, all business as usual.

"Release forms signed, sponsor reads prepped, and maybe don't libel a haunted Raggedy Ann, thanks." He pointed at me. "Also: BTS vlog. Viewers love mess. And Shaunie?"

"Yes, Dad?"

"If you're gonna tease soulmate stuff, at least promise a love-themed reading with Esme. It'll chart on socials."

I drew a heart and stabbed it with an arrow. "Done. I'll script questions."

Harrison stacked his notes, perfectly squared. "And I'll compile actual research."

"Yin and yang," Marty sang. "Just wait until you two see the Sage Hollow Inn," he added, leaning one shoulder against the doorframe. "Haunted as hell. It's gonna make for great content."

"See?" I turned to Harrison, my pulse humming with excitement. "Haunted as *hell*. This is gonna be epic."

"Or a disaster." Harrison pushed his notes into a neat stack, because of course he did. "Creaky pipes. Drafty windows. Lagging Wi-Fi signal."

Marty raised his brows. "Listeners eat that up. Ghost tourism is like pumpkin spice. It always sells."

I grinned. "Exactly. Pumpkin spice and prophecies, baby."

Harrison groaned. "Why do I feel like that's our next merch slogan?"

"Because it is."

Marty snorted into his coffee. "I'd buy that."

I leaned back in my chair, the adrenaline of recording finally bleeding off. "I need to add my crystal collection to my packing list."

"You're not seriously bringing crystals," Harrison muttered.

"Of course, I am. What if the inn is *seriously* haunted? You'll be begging for a protection stone by night two."

"I'll take a surge protector over a protection stone."

Marty laughed again. "Add the crystal thing to your behind-the-scenes vlog. People would eat it up."

"Already planning on it." I tapped my pumpkin mug like it was a gavel. "Shaunie's Guide to Surviving a

Haunted Inn: Step one, don't taunt the dolls. Step two, bring snacks."

"Step three," Harrison said dryly, "lower your expectations."

I rolled my eyes. "Spoken like a man who's never had a ghost crawl into bed with him."

"Because ghosts don't crawl into beds," he said, exasperated. "Drafts do. Squeaky mattresses do. Overactive imaginations do."

Marty waggled his eyebrows. "If it squeaks, don't come complainin' to me."

I groaned. "You're both impossible."

But as Marty chuckled and Harrison fought another twitch of a smile, the studio suddenly felt too still. The red *ON AIR* light flickered even though it was already off. For a second, I swore I heard a soft scratching in the walls, like nails dragging across insulation.

I froze, heart thudding. "Did you hear that?" I whispered.

Harrison blinked at me, deadpan. "Probably the building settling."

"Or Annabelle saying hi." Marty's grin was mischievous, but his eyes darted to the wall too.

I shivered, bracelets chiming as I gathered my things. Whether it was faulty wiring or us conjuring Annabelle simply by talking about her, I wasn't about to hang around and find out.

Marty seemed to have the same idea because he made toward the exit, "Don't get killed before we get to New Hampshire."

"No promises," I shouted. "Harry's just waiting for his opportunity to take me out." I slashed a finger across my throat, tilted my head to the side, and stuck out my tongue.

Being alone with my co-host left a sort of charge in the air.

Harrison picked up his iPad. "You know you don't have to fill every silence with a joke, Siobhan, right?"

He always used my full name as a retort to me calling him Harry, except I didn't hate it the way he did. Of course, I couldn't let him know that, though, or he would stop. For some reason, I liked the way it sounded coming from him. And he pronounced it correctly, so that was a win. I'd ended up with my nickname simply because I got tired of having to correct everyone who butchered my real name.

My laugh came out softer than intended. "Says the man who fills every feeling with a statistic."

A truce of a look passed between us—brief, fragile—and then he nodded. "See you later." He swung open the door. "Don't let the doll get you. I can't do this show alone."

I covered my chest with my hand and let out a gasp. "Is that an actual compliment, Mr. Moretti?"

He scoffed. "Don't flatter yourself. I don't have the energy to break in a new co-host."

I hollered after him as he exited, "You can admit you like me, Harry. I won't bite." The door slammed, closing me into the soundproof coffin. "Well, I *might* bite, but not hard." After grabbing my things, I exited the studio to find Winnie stretching her back with a yawn, then she froze, stared into the far corner, and hissed.

"Nope," I told the emptiness, scooping up my cat and plopping her into her carrier. "Absolutely not today, Satan... or Raggedy Ann."

I flicked off the lights and the neon exit sign washed everything red. My reflection ghosted in the dark studio window—blurred, doubled, slightly off. I pressed two fingers to the glass.

They came away cold.

TWO

By the time we hit the New Hampshire border, the sky had put on its moody fall sweater. Gray knit. A little frayed at the edges. Every tree we passed looked like it had swallowed a sunset and refused to burp it back up; reds so dramatic they bordered on messy lipstick, yellows bright enough to make a highlighter jealous. It'd been uncharacteristically warm that fall, prolonging the leaf-peeping season well into October.

Winnie blinked at me from her backpack carrier on the passenger seat like I'd personally invented car travel just to offend her. She'd tolerated the first hour, tolerated the second hour slightly less, and was now on the cusp of composing a formal complaint with our non-existent HR department. You'd think she'd be used to traveling since she'd accompanied me on countless adventures over the years, but she had the stereotypical calico cat-itude.

"Five bucks says the inn's haunted by a disgruntled chambermaid named Mildred," I announced, taking the turn into Sage Hollow. The welcome sign was hand-painted in the kind of cursive that looked like it smelled nice. If it was scratch-and-sniff, it would definitely waft apple pie and cinnamon.

"Mildred?" Harrison interrupted through my car's Bluetooth.

"Yes. She rattles bead curtains at midnight and demands back pay in peppermint candies."

"Statistically speaking," Harrison said, like the killjoy he is, "most 'hauntings' are plumbing."

"Wow, you're fun," I muttered, but my lips curled.

We caravanned because I insisted on driving, Harrison insisted on *not* getting in a car I was driving, and Marty's car was too packed with equipment for additional passengers. At least I got to lead because I'd won the coin toss. My crystals, several bundles of sage, a spray bottle of holy water, an EMF reader to detect spirit activity, and entirely too many sweaters were shoved into my two suitcases (a girl needs options) in the back of my Subaru. Harrison followed in his practical sedan, which I was willing to bet had no more than one small bag in the trunk. Marty was a few miles behind us because he'd stopped for coffee number three and a pumpkin muffin "for the brand." When the road narrowed to one lane and the trees leaned in as if they had secrets to spill, I rolled down my window. The air tasted like balsam fir and apples.

The town of Sage Hollow appeared all at once, like it had been waiting to welcome us with a rolled out red carpet. Middle Hollow Road was a perfect movie set: clapboard storefronts with black trim, window boxes overflowing with mums, a scarecrow family posed on a bench like they were patiently waiting their turn at the DMV. A banner overhead signaled we were heading the right direction. *SAGE HOLLOW HARVEST WEEK* was written in pumpkin-orange with tiny witch hats dotting each corner.

"Try not to run over any decorative gourds," Harrison said, pulling in behind me as I parked in front of a shop whose sign read, *Ever After Emporium*, with a crescent moon dangling from the first E. In the window hung another hand-lettered sign: *Home of Esme*, and below that, *World-Renowned Medium Matchmaker*.

"Keep your skepticism holstered," I warned, unbuckling Winnie's carrier straps and slinging her onto my back. "Esme is a legend."

"She advertises soulmates next to soy candles."

"Multitasking." I turned off my ignition and grabbed my phone from the holder on my dash. "Also, candles are a love language. Hanging up now." I ended the call, got out, and shut my car door with my hip. It was a few degrees cooler than the fifty-seven-degree weather we'd left behind in Boston, so I zipped up my candy apple-red vest and adjusted my pumpkin beanie.

Harrison stepped onto the sidewalk in a dark flannel, the green making his eyes look deeper, moodier. A *Gargoyles* tee peeked out beside the open buttons because of course it did. He glanced at my beanie. "You're wearing seasonal produce."

"You're wearing a cartoon rock," I shot back.

His gaze dipped to my hand. Or, more specifically, the keyring I was holding. "That's going to break your ignition. Why do you need so many?"

"Because I do," I huffed. I'd been collecting keychains since the day I'd gotten my license. To keep me safe, my parents gave me a four-leaf clover preserved in resin that they'd had my aunt send over from Ireland. The next one was a (questionably yellow) stuffed Tweety Bird I'd bought on my senior trip to Six Flags New England. After that, my college crest printed on plastic. Then—

The bell over Esme's door jingled as I pushed inside, and for a second, I had that weightless feeling you get when an elevator starts to rise, like the room was moving and I would catch up in a second. The air was warm and sweet with sap; incense braided with the clean bite of rosemary oil. Crystals tucked into vintage teacups lined one wall and decks of tarot and oracle cards were displayed beneath glass cloches on another. A royal-blue velvet sofa lounged in the front window, drowning in pillows embroidered with evil eyes.

Esme herself stood tall behind the counter like she'd been expecting us all morning. Her shimmering silver hair fell to her waist in a thick braid, and her eyes were the exact color of the river rock bracelets on her wrists. She wore a black wrap dress embroidered with metallic-silver spirals around the neckline. Her vibe suggested she was a chic witch who would not tolerate any attitude.

"Harrison." Her lips curved into a genuine smile. It was the kind a sweet grandmother would offer as she served you lemonade. "Siobhan," she said, pronouncing it correctly without a blink. It hit me like stepping out of a cold shadow and into sunlight. "Welcome to Sage Hollow."

"You said my name right," I blurted, then immediately considered flinging myself into a display of rose quartz to hide. "Sorry. That's rare."

"Names matter," Esme said. "They're an invitation."

Harrison made a polite noise, the kind you make at a wake when someone tells a joke you didn't catch. He kept his hands in his pockets like he was afraid to accidentally touch anything and get hexed.

Marty arrived a beat later with a gust of cold air and a to-go tray like a peace offering. "I come bearing caffeine and contracts." He extended a paper cup to me—a PSL, bless him.

"We're honored to have you," Esme said. "Shall we do the sit-down in the reading room?"

"Yasss," I replied, because who doesn't love a reading room? Also, because my brain is ninety percent confetti. But seriously, a room just for reading...like, what?! I followed her through a beaded doorway (*Mildred, is that you?*) into a space that looked like a midnight picnic. A round table. Six chairs. Deep blue walls pricked with framed constellations. Candles (not the cheap ones, the good ones) flickered in star-shaped holders. Books filled the shelves that encompassed the room, and I desperately wanted to take my time going through them all.

Winnie went boneless in her carrier with a dramatic sigh that translated to: *I'd like to speak to your manager*. I spun the backpack around, placing it on my lap as I sat, and opened the mesh so she could peek out. She blinked, decided Esme wasn't a threat, and proceeded to ignore our existence like any self-respecting cat.

"And who is this?" Esme gestured toward my lap.

"This is my emotional barometer, Winnie, for short. Winifred, for long."

She tipped her chin. "Pleasure to meet you, Winifred. I am a fan of Bette Midler, myself."

A smile lit up my face. "You know *Hocus Pocus*?"

She flipped her dress over her knees as she settled into the chair to my left. "I live in the Halloween capital of America. How could I not know of it?"

Harrison took the seat opposite me and balanced his iPad on the edge of the table like a tether to reality. "Salem, Massachusetts might disagree with you there."

Esme let out a laugh that, coming from anyone but her,

would've sounded engineered for the role of *mystical witch*. "Yes, our southern neighbor does like to stand atop the pedestal. After your stay here, you can decide who deserves the crown."

Marty set up a discreet mic on a stand. "Level check," he said, tapping one headphone. "Esme, can I get a line?"

"Of course." Esme's voice was smoke over honey. "Welcome to the liminal."

Marty grinned. "Hot." He scooted papers toward Esme. "We need you to sign these release forms before we begin."

I sipped my PSL, trying to swallow the nerves down with it, while Esme flipped through the contract. This was the kind of space that made you whisper even though you weren't supposed to whisper. The kind of room that felt like it knew you. Part library; part Akashic Records.

Once Esme had signed, Marty gave me the go-ahead to begin.

"So." I cleared my throat. "For our listeners, and for Harrison, what exactly is a Medium Matchmaker?"

Esme's eyes brightened. "Labels are for jars, my dear. But if we must: I listen. The living. The dead. The threads between them. We get tangled. I help untangle."

Harrison's posture didn't bend, but his attention did. "You make predictions?"

"I offer possibilities." Her smile deepened. "Choice is the magic."

I rested my arms on the table and leaned over Winnie. "How did you get so famous that people come from all over to ask you to fix their love lives?"

"I don't *fix*, Siobhan. I simply point in the right direction." Her eyes darted to Harrison before landing on me once more. "As for how I became *famous*, as you say, well,

I'm good at what I do, and word spread fast." She twirled a finger in the air. "Halloween capital."

"Speaking of..." My chest did that hummingbird thing it does when I'm about to do something reckless. "You probably know this, but dating apps are atrocious—"

"Not this again," Harrison grumbled.

I stuck my tongue out at him.

Marty made the universal keep-it-going motion.

I fiddled with my rings and continued, "I teased on our show that you might help me find my soulmate."

Esme rested her hands on the table, palms up. Her bracelets clunked against the hard wood hidden beneath the ornate tapestry. "Do you want a card pull, Siobhan? Or shall we go straight to the part you came for?"

"The part I came for," I said, before my filter could put on shoes.

Her lashes lowered. She was quiet so long I could hear Winnie's soft sleepy purr. The candle flames licked higher, bending toward Esme like flowers to the sun. Harrison's fingers tightened on his iPad, a small, betraying tell. He could play the skeptic act all he wanted, but I suspected he was more curious about the occult than he let on. Otherwise, why would he have wanted to work for our podcast in the first place? Let alone agree to *co-host* it. Riddle me that.

Esme lifted her gaze and pinned me with it. Not mean. Not even intense. Exact. "There is a kiss waiting for you," she said. "One kiss before All Hallows' Eve will change everything."

It was a simple sentence, but it hit me like a door opening somewhere I hadn't noticed. I clutched the rose quartz crystal that was dangling around my neck.

"Define *everything*," Harrison said, the corner of his

mouth tugging. He was trying for amused. It landed closer to rattled.

"Everything is one of those words that means what it says." Esme's eyes didn't leave mine.

The prospect of my entire life changing had me spinning the rings on my finger incessantly until the skin beneath became irritated. Sure, my life was chaotic and *might* benefit from certain changes, but it was *my* chaos. "Cool, cool, love that for me," I said, too brightly. "It's giving...super casual destiny."

Harrison glanced at Marty like *for the love of God* and then at me—really at me—for half a second, and I felt unsteady in my chair. He looked away first.

"Can we give that another go?" Marty asked, businesslike again, because he is both a chaos goblin and a professional. "We can tease the Halloween special with it."

"Of course," Esme said. "Truth is designed to be heard, after all."

We recorded a bite for the episode with Esme repeating the line about the kiss, me making an appropriately flustered noise, Harrison injecting a comment about 'self-fulfilling prophecies' that would get the skeptics riled up in the comments. When Marty was satisfied, he exclaimed, "That's golden."

"Now." Esme stood. "Let's get you settled."

"The inn?" I asked, already picturing creaky floors and floral wallpaper and a ghost named Mildred who collected thimbles.

"The inn has been expecting you." She said it like the building had sent a save-the-date.

We stepped back out onto Middle Hollow Road. Harrison held the door for me; I pretended not to notice. Marty fell into step with Esme like a duckling following a glamorous pond witch. I had to hand it to her; there was something absolutely magnetic about that woman.

"Can you just leave your place empty?" Harrison asked as we followed her up the road.

She flicked her wrist. "I'll only be gone for a spell. Archie will keep watch for me."

"Archie?" I asked, not recalling seeing another person there.

"Yes. He was a coachman here in the early eighteen-hundreds who fancies hanging around my shop," she said matter-of-factly, as though it was completely normal to leave her store in the hands of a centuries-old ghost.

"Oh. I would love to meet Archie next time we stop by," I replied, because what the heck else was I supposed to say?

Harrison grabbed my arm, bringing us to a halt, and making Winnie hiss. "Damn cat," he muttered.

"She wouldn't hate you if you actually bothered to spend time with her, you know."

Marty and Esme continued, leaving several yards between us.

"Do you really want to risk our show's reputation on this quack?" Harrison whispered.

I shook my arm free. "She's a medium. Her job involves talking to the dead. I'm not sure why you're surprised by that."

He rolled his eyes as he moved into step beside me. "We push a lot of boundaries on this show for ratings, but do you want to hang what will be our most streamed episode of the season, on the word of a woman who leaves a figment of her imagination in charge of her livelihood?"

I patted his shoulder, which was firmer than it looked. "Live a little, Harry. Besides, if this all turns out to be a sham, you'll get to say, 'told you so,' and we all know how much you love saying that don't we Winnie?"

She mewed on cue.

"Ooo, look. A cider cart," I exclaimed, clapping my hands, as I pointed across the street to an alleyway between the shops.

"A huh," Harrison replied, his voice full of disinterest, but I caught his lips curling up in one corner before he turned away.

The Sage Hollow Inn appeared at the end of the street where it sat on a slight rise. It was a three-story, white-painted, Victorian-style manor with dark green shutters. It had a porch, adorned with pumpkins and hay bales, wrapped around it like a protective arm. A wooden placard swung from the black iron gate: *Sage Hollow Inn Est. 1858.* Someone had threaded a tiny bouquet of dried sage through the chain.

I nudged Harrison with my elbow. "It's giving murder mystery weekend."

"It's giving outdated wiring," he mocked.

Inside smelled like clove oil, old books, and a history that didn't apologize. The foyer housed an explosion of antiques. An umbrella stand carved like a fox stood in one corner, a gilt mirror (that may have trapped at least one soul on a Tuesday) hung above a velvet bench, and a grand-mother clock ticked beside the stairs in that stately way clocks tick when they know you can't stop them.

The innkeeper—Betty, according to her name tag— looked like pie just came out of her oven and she was pleased about it. "Welcome," she said. "You must be the podcast people." She said *podcast* the way other people say *tattoo*: curious, a touch wary, yet open to being convinced.

"That's us," Marty said, sliding his producer smile into place.

Esme handed Betty some kind of card, which the innkeeper tucked into her apron. "This is where I bid you adieu. I can assure you that you are in good hands here."

"Thank you," I said with a wave that made my bangles jingle. "And thanks for the prophecy. I'll be sure to exfoliate my lips extra well tonight." I cringed to hold in a groan. *Why am I so awkward?*

"We're all set to check in?" Marty asked Betty once Esme left.

The older woman's smile did a thing. Not shrinking, exactly. More like...careful. "Well," she said. "We've had a little situation."

Harrison's shoulders squared. "What kind of situation?"

"Nothing to worry over," Betty rushed. "It's just Harvest Week is busier than expected, and we've had, oh, dear, a plumbing hiccup in the west wing." She folded her hands as if bracing for a verdict. "We can't use those rooms until the pipes stop throwing tantrums."

Harrison leaned toward me and whispered, "I predicted problematic plumbing. Does that mean I can start prophesizing?"

Before he pulled away, I caught a whiff of his scent. Cedar, bergamot, and soap. Clean. Very on brand.

Marty glanced at us. "Okay. What does that mean for our rooms?"

"It means," Betty said so sweetly one would be hard-pressed to argue, "You, Martin, will be staying in my quilting room. There is a very comfortable pull-out sofa bed in there." She turned her attention to Harrison and me. "And you two will be in the Honeymoon Suite."

My laugh tripped and fell on its face. "I'm sorry; the what?"

Betty brightened, relieved to finally give someone good news. "It's our nicest room. Top floor. Fireplace. Clawfoot tub. Very romantic." She lowered her voice as if the potted fern might be a gossip. "The suite prefers couples."

"The suite prefers..." I repeated, then threw a look at Harrison that probably could have curdled milk. "We're not a couple."

"Statistically unlikely," Harrison agreed, which was not the point.

"As Esme would say, suites don't care about labels," Betty quipped.

"We booked two rooms," Harrison said, practical to the marrow. "Two keys. Two beds. Zero shared suites."

Betty winced. "I'm truly sorry. Between the festival and the, er, pipes, the Honeymoon Suite is what we have. But it's spacious." Her eyes flicked toward me, then to Harrison, and then back like she was trying to decide if we were the kind of people who would appreciate free cookies. "There's a screen you can unfold between the bed and the sitting room where there's a lovely chaise."

The silence stretched like taffy. The grandmother clock counted out several heavy seconds. A faint cinnamon scent wafted passed but it was gone nearly as suddenly as it had entered.

Marty rubbed his forehead with two fingers, already calculating clicks. "We can make it work," he said, because he is the devil. "From a content perspective, it's actually—"

"Don't say 'golden,'" I hissed as I furiously spun my fidget ring.

"—golden." The jerk beamed.

"The only person I'm meant to be sharing a room with tonight is Mildred and her beaded curtains," I lamented.

"Who's Mildred?" Marty furrowed his bushy brows.

"The chambermaid," I whined, the decibel of my tone approaching sound barrier-breaking levels.

"It's fine," Harrison said, in that careful voice he uses when he is trying very hard not to react to my chaos. His jaw tightened. He looked at me, not past me or around me, just at me, and something in my spine aligned like a zipper. "We're adults. We'll manage a room."

Betty exhaled like a kettle coming off the boil. "Wonderful! I'll bring extra towels." She plucked a pair of brass keys off a hook. "You're on the third floor behind the door labeled *Honeymoon Suite.*" She handed me one key, Harrison the other. "Oh, and if you hear odd sounds after midnight, it's just the pipes, unless you believe that haunted hullabaloo."

"Plumbing," Harrison said, reassured by the lie.

"Mildred," I muttered like an obstinate child as I curled my fingers around the cool weight of the key. The tag was heart-shaped because of course it was. I glanced at Harrison again, at the stubborn set of his mouth and the stupid sexy curl at his temple. How was I meant to find my soulmate if I was shacked up with Harrison the Horrible all week?

"Pumpkin spice and prophecies," I punctuated with a sigh, because if I didn't make a joke I might actually self-combust. The comforting satisfaction of my PSL had completely worn off at the words, *honeymoon suite.* "Betty, where can I find the nearest coffee shop?"

THREE

I clutched the folding screen like it was a diplomatic flag. "Demilitarized zone?"

Harrison unfolded it with the solemnity of a judge and set it between the bed and the chaise. "Boundaries," he said, like a man who alphabetizes his spice rack. "You take the bed. I'll take the chaise."

"Yes, that's a gentleman's chaise," I said decisively, as though I had spawned the idea, completely disregarding the pink ruffles.

"It's a chaise." He draped his flannel over the back like he was claiming territory in a national park. At least it disguised some of the furniture's frills.

Winnie hopped onto the equally pink floral duvet, kneaded a Switzerland-sized circle, and flopped with a sigh that translated to *everyone behave.* I set a smoky quartz on the nightstand beside the heart-shaped key, which glinted under the lamp, then I lit my sage bundle and began smudging the suite.

Harrison poked his head around the divider. "This place doesn't smell musty enough, you've got to add to it?"

I clicked my tongue. "Tsk, tsk. Do you want the energy of honeymooners past to be lingering while we sleep?"

He groaned, but ceased protesting, which was about as close to acceptance as I'd get from him.

After I'd sufficiently cleansed the space, I blotted out my sage and retrieved a black obsidian crystal from my metaphysical toolkit. "Knock, knock," I called from my side of the screen.

"Yes?" he grumbled.

"May I come in?" I rolled up and down on my toes.

"Shaunie, you just walked around the whole room, intent on smoking us out. *Now* you want to honor boundaries?"

"Valid." I stepped around the divider and held out my outstretched hand. "Here. Put this under your pillow."

He glanced at the stone, then up at me. "You want me to sleep on a rock?"

I gripped his wrist, tugging until his palm faced out, then deposited the obsidian there. "I don't want to hear you cry when this place gives you nightmares tonight, so just do it."

His fingers closed around the crystal. "Whatever."

"I'll take that," I replied as I dropped his arm, then I scooted around to my side. "Do you want to use the bathroom first?"

"Go ahead."

The bathroom was in the neutral zone. After I finished, I wasted no time getting into bed before he could see my custom Halloween cat jammies, which had Winnie's face topped with a witch hat printed on them.

"You're up," I hollered once I was safely tucked in.

Not even a minute later, the bathroom door clicked closed. It didn't take him very long.

"Lights?" he asked, once he emerged.

"Go for it."

Darkness pressed in, and the suite did its best haunted-house impression. The radiator knocked in what I'm fairly certain was Morse code for *run*, the pipes whispered to each other about our life choices, and once my eyes adjusted, it appeared as though the floral wallpaper stared like a thousand nosy aunties.

Through the screen, Harrison's voice came soft, "For the record, if you get spooked, wake me. I'm not interested in explaining your broken ankle to Marty."

"That was almost sweet," I whispered.

"Statistically prudent."

I smiled into my pillow where no one could see. "'Night, Harry."

"Good night, Siobhan."

SOMETHING CLANKED inside the wall behind my headboard around two a.m. It was a shy little tap like a pipe trying to cough up a ghost. Winnie's ears went radar. Then three bangs, evenly spaced, in a distinctive triangle. My brain labeled it *Mildred*; my goose bumped skin labeled it *not plumbing*. I reached toward the nightstand, knocked the key, and it pinged against the wood floor like a tiny bell. The screen rustled.

"You okay?" Harrison asked, voice sleep-rough, closer than the screen should've allowed.

A draft brushed my cheek. "Totally fine," I whispered, not moving. "The suite and I are just...negotiating."

He let out a huff that might've been a laugh. "Wake me if it escalates."

"It already did. I named the radiator Mildred."

"Plumbing," he said, but gently this time.

The suite went quiet. Winnie settled. I wondered about the actual newlyweds who must've stayed in that room over the years. The wallpaper caught my attention again. *If only those little flowers could talk...*

BY MORNING, the Honeymoon Suite had not murdered us.

It tried, don't get me wrong, but it had not succeeded. Thanks to my sage and crystals, no doubt. I decided not being murdered was as good an omen as any, so I bribed Harrison with the promise of strong Wi-Fi somewhere in town and we set out to locate caffeine that didn't come from Betty's antique carafe.

Sage Hollow at nine a.m. was a postcard with a pulse. Kids in overalls chased each other around hay bales stacked into a smiling pumpkin tower. A fiddler on the corner played something sprightly enough to make my feet twitch. The banner for *SAGE HOLLOW HARVEST WEEK* rippled like a witch's skirt in the breeze.

The coffee shop had a bell that did *not* jingle, rather it clonked like a cowbell calling the livestock home for dinner. The chalkboard sign outside Black Cat Coffee Co. promised maple lattes, cider donuts, and my personal saving grace, pumpkin spice. A chalk ghost on the sidewalk wore sunglasses, and I loved it immediately.

"Statistically speaking," Harrison said, pushing open the door for me, "the louder the bell, the worse the espresso."

"Everything is a statistic with you." I brushed past him. "I bet you're fun at parties."

Inside, a warm, sugary cloud of baked apples and

espresso hung in the air. The bar was an old church pew, and the menu was written in curly script on black slate. A girl with bat-wing eyeliner worked the machine like a tiny, caffeinated wizard.

"You think I can pull off that eyeliner?" I polled Harrison while we waited in line.

"I don't think she'd appreciate you tugging on her eyelids, but you can try."

I blinked. "Did you just crack a joke?"

He shrugged. That was it. A single shrug.

When it was our turn, I ordered my usual along with two cider donuts. Harrison asked for a black coffee because of course he did. Winnie peered over the edge of her backpack carrier from my shoulders and hiss-yawned, which is cat for, "don't talk to me before noon." *I feel, ya, kitty.*

We claimed a small table near the window. Marty shuffled in a minute later, wind-chapped and triumphant, holding up a permit like a trophy. "Clearance for later," he announced. "You two look almost human."

"High praise," my roomie uttered.

Bat-Wing delivered our order, and Harrison swallowed a grimly satisfied sip. "Acceptable."

I took a bite of donut that made my soul tap-dance. I licked sugar from my thumb, leaned into the table, and, because self-control is a myth I believe in about as much as I believe in sugar-free brownies, slid straight into confetti-brain.

"So," I said, voice low and conspiratorial. "One kiss. Before All Hallows' Eve."

"Must you workshop your destiny before I'm sufficiently caffeinated?" Harrison grumbled.

Marty wiggled his brows. "For the record, the prophecy

bite...chef's kiss. The internet loves a good romance storyline."

"Speaking of kisses," I said, because I am a menace, "what if the suite—"

"Do not personify the suite," Harrison said.

"—sets the stage for fate." I continued, ignoring him. "It prefers *couples*, Harry."

"Pipes prefer maintenance," he countered, but the corner of his mouth tugged and I felt stupidly brave.

I didn't realize I'd said the next part too loudly until the woman behind us gasped.

"I am so sorry," she blurted, leaning around our table with an expression I can only describe as *I Brought Cookies and Also Destiny*. She wore a pumpkin-orange cardigan with tiny leaf buttons and had the kind of hair that looked like it remembered perms fondly. I liked her immediately. "I didn't mean to eavesdrop, but did you say a prophecy about a kiss?"

Harrison closed his eyes like he was making a wish for patience.

I put on my brightest YouTube personality smile. "I did say that. Hi. I'm—"

"Shaunie," she said proudly. "You're the podcast girl! My daughter and I listen while she's doing PTA duties. I'm Lynnette Wakefield." She extended a hand toward Harrison without looking away from me. "And you must be the skeptic."

"Occupational hazard," he said dryly, shaking once.

Lynnette clutched her tote like it contained state secrets. "Well, I'm not one to meddle—"

Marty let out a barely audible snort.

"—but if there's a kiss that's supposed to change every-thing, I would feel personally remiss if I didn't introduce you to my son." She rummaged furiously through her purse and produced her phone like a magician with a rabbit. "Dalton. He's twenty-nine. Helps run the family orchard. Coaches youth soccer. Volunteers for the festival committee. Has health insurance."

"Hot," I said, before my brain could file that under *Inside Thoughts*. My thumb went to my fidget ring and gave it a few turns.

Lynnette swiped to another photo. Dalton, leaning on a truck bed, smiling with his whole face and a smear of paint on one forearm. The kind of square-jawed handsome that makes your grandmother sigh. There was also a dog with its front paws perched on Dalton's thigh like *I, too, am a good boy*.

"That's Patch," Lynnette said, the proudest of moms. "Sweetest thing alive. My sister breeds Golden Retrievers."

Winnie made an offended sound behind me.

Marty leaned over my arm, shameless. "We love a dog. Our audience loves a dog."

"Our audience loves my cat," I countered, my voice hushed.

Harrison's jaw did that tic thing. "We're not a reality dating show."

"Of course," Lynnette said, unfazed. "But sometimes the universe leaves the door open and it's bad manners not to peek."

I took a breath that tasted like cinnamon sugar and possibility and bad ideas. "What's Dalton's schedule like this week?"

Harrison stared at me as if I'd announced I was eloping with a scarecrow. "Siobhan."

Marty clapped his hands softly, producer brain already

doing a jig. "Tomorrow night? Quick coffee date? Tasteful B-roll?"

Lynnette beamed as if she'd fixed the economy. "He's free after six once the pumpkin patch closes. He can meet you right here. He can bring Patch."

"Wait. Did you say pumpkin patch? And his dog's name is Patch?" Harrison quipped.

Lynnette, not fazed in the least by my co-host's 'tude, replied, "Why, yes. Where do you think Patch got his name?"

"Perfect," Marty said, because he is the devil dressed like my friend.

"A dog in a coffee shop?" Harrison asked, seizing on logistics like a life preserver. "That is named after a cat?"

"Patio," Lynnette said, already texting. "They have heaters out there. He'll be delighted. He loves fall. And pretty women. But mostly fall."

I laughed, helplessly.

Harrison looked at me, at the donut sugar on my thumb, at Winnie's judgmental ears, at Lynnette vibrating like a speaker at an EDM concert, and then at Marty who was practically salivating at the thought of ratings, no doubt. He set his coffee down with the resignation of a man who knows he cannot stop a tidal wave with a cardboard coaster. "For the record," he declared, "if this goes sideways, I reserve the right to say, 'I told you so' into a microphone."

"You always reserve that right," I said. "You *laminate* that right."

Lynnette's phone dinged. She glanced down, then up with another delighted squeal. "He says he's in."

Something told me this mama wouldn't let her son say no, regardless. Something unsteady slid under my ribs.

"Romance in a coffee house," Marty whispered, scribbling notes.

Harrison tried not to smile and failed, barely, but I caught it. "Siobhan," he said, softer. "Just be careful."

It landed too close to warm, so I made a face to keep my insides from showing. "I have a cat, a pumpkin beanie, and three crystals in my bra. I am invincible."

We set the time for this first date with my soulmate at six. Lynnette refused to let us pay for our drinks (small-town hospitality) and squeezed my hands like she was passing me a blessing. The bell clonked as she left, and I felt the room resettle like snow in a shaken globe.

Marty clasped his hands together. "Okay, team. We're going to do this gently. No ambush, no bits. We let it be whatever it is. If it's cute? Great. If it's awkward? Great. If it's a disaster? Possibly better."

"Content goblin," I teased.

"Storyteller," he corrected.

Harrison flipped his iPad around, so the screen faced me. He'd already pulled up a notes doc titled *Dalton Date: Boundaries/Questions* because of course he had. "Ground rules," he said. "No talk of prophecies unless he brings it up. No promises you can't keep. If at any point you feel uncomfortable, we leave. No content is worth you being hurt." He swallowed.

Something in my chest did that *zip* thing again. "Copy," I said, aiming for flippant and landing closer to grateful. "I'll let you handle the questions."

He clicked his pen once. "Obviously you won't."

"Obvi," I agreed with a grin, and ate the second donut to stop my face from doing anything suspicious.

Outside, a gust of wind sent a swirl of leaves skittering

down Middle Hollow Road and the banner snapped its little witch hats. Winnie released a reluctant purr that translated to: *Fine, chaos. But do it cute.*

Marty gestured out the window. "Let's get some establishing shots around town and then swing by the inn for B-roll. I bet the suite loves a close-up."

"Don't personify the suite," Harrison and I said at the same time—him, serious; me, mocking.

We stared at each other for a heartbeat longer than necessary, and something bright and terrifying skittered across my skin like static.

I broke eye contact first, because if Esme was right and I had this fuse that was simply waiting for a spark, I wasn't about to let *Harrison* hand me matches.

"To pumpkin spice and prophecies," I said, raising my paper cup.

Harrison rolled his eyes. "Your frequent use of that phrase has me concerned."

"Don't hate because you're jealous you didn't come up with it." I flicked my hair over my shoulder.

"Jealous? No. I'm concerned you're going to turn it into our theme song."

"I'm sorry. Is the grown man wearing a *Flintstones* tee afraid of a theme song?"

Marty lifted his cup. "You know, pumpkin spice and prophecies would be a great name for the episode."

"Thanks, Dad." I stuck my tongue out at my co-host, earning me one of his signature groans.

The bell clonked again as another customer came in, and somewhere under the chatter and milk frother hiss, I could've sworn I heard a faint, familiar click-click from old pipes.

Plumbing, I told myself.

Possibility, whispered the part of me that had already started exfoliating my lips.

By late afternoon, Sage Hollow switched on a golden-hour filter that made everything look cinematic. Even the cracked sidewalks. Marty said something about "establishing shots" and "opening credits" as if we were the budget version of prestige TV, and then handed Harrison a coil of XLR like it was a relay baton.

We'd spent the early part of the day collecting B-roll: porch pumpkins, a scarecrow family that changed positions every time I blinked (rude), the cider cart that I had yet to check out, but it was on my list. After, we headed toward the famously haunted Saint Benedict's Cemetery, small and old, tucked just off Middle Hollow Road like the town had been built around it.

The iron gate had that curly, wrought flourish that said *I was here when your great-greats were comparing pie recipes.* In my head, it sounded like Cogsworth. Talking clock...talking gate. Fallen leaves crunched underfoot, and the headstones were the thin slate kind with winged skulls and names that felt like spells: Temperance, Mercy, Eleazer. Someone had left a sprig of rosemary on a grave. According to my book, *The Witch's Guide to Herbs*, it symbolized the immortality of the soul.

"Okay," Marty said, doing his little conductor hands. "We keep it respectful, we keep it quiet, we keep it sexy." He paused. "Not like—no, I don't mean that kind of sexy. I mean tasteful, spooky. Like a cashmere ghost."

"A what," Harrison said flatly.

"A cashmere ghost," Marty repeated, as if that explained anything. He adjusted the equipment on the small folding table that constituted our makeshift sound-stage, nestled between one Clarence Jeffries, 1842 to 1897, and one Marion Lovett? Lovell? Circa 1820-something? Her headstone was worse for wear, making it difficult to decipher.

"Shaunie." Marty handed me my body pack with the lavalier mic cord already plugged into it. After clipping the transmitter to the back of my jeans, I fed the wire up under my clothes and affixed the tiny microphone to my vest, taking note of the small crowd of tourists and a few locals (only twenty-four hours in that town and I could tell the difference) who had gathered along the gravel path. Harrison would be cursing up a storm about the crunching sounds beneath everyone's boots that he'd have to remove in post.

A familiar face smiled at me and waved with enough enthusiasm to make my cheeks match the color of Sage Hollow's prized empire apples. I raised my hand toward Lynnette, then dropped it just as quickly. *Should I really be this unnerved by my future mother-in-law?*

Potential. *Potential* mother-in-law. I'd liked her when we'd met in the coffee shop earlier, but since that morning, I'd barely stopped thinking about Dalton and the prophecy, so the pressure was on. It always was whenever I decided to date. I was often too much for guys to handle. Too much for most people, if I was being honest. That'd been my curse all my life, which was why I kept my distance from living beings besides Winnie. She was next to the table, secured in her backpack carrier, eyeing a child in the crowd. More specifically, the child's apple cider donut. Winnie had a sweet tooth, like her mama.

Lynnette nudged a bottle-blonde woman beside her, her bestie, if I had to guess, and they both waved at me. Right. I'd been talking about my mother-in-law before I was derailed. Sometimes, my train took a wrong turn out of the station, but I always found my way back. Usually.

So, potentially, I could be Lynnette's daughter-in-law one day. I was already picturing us swapping pie recipes on Thanksgiving. From the research I'd done on Esme, one thing was for certain: the woman didn't miss. That meant, before the week was up, I was going to kiss my soulmate. Well, I suppose she hadn't said it *quite* like that, but I'd read between the lines, okay? So, according to the girl math I'd pulled together throughout the day, that meant there was a high statistical probability that I was the future Mrs. Dalton Wakefield.

Ugh, when did I start sounding like Harrison? We needed to vacate the honeymoon suite ASAP. I made a mental note to discuss it with Betty that evening. Then, knowing I would forget because...well, me...I fished my notebook out of my bag and scribbled the reminder on a blank page.

Marty clasped his hands together and nodded toward our guest. Esme had been waiting beneath a sugar maple whose remaining leaves blazed orange. She'd swapped her wrap dress for a long black coat and a scarf the color of twilight. Her braid was pinned up, and silver hoops hung from her ears. Somehow, she made the world look like *it* had dressed to meet her.

"Thank you for arranging access," Harrison said as she approached our table because, although a skeptic, he was also a Boy Scout.

"Saint Benedict's always says yes to good manners," Esme replied. "And to muffins left on the rectory steps." Her eyes warmed when they landed on me. "Siobhan."

It still did something to me, hearing it right. Like finding my name on a souvenir keychain for once. I adjusted my beanie (pumpkin, again—brand synergy) and lowered my voice automatically, the way you do in hospitals and holy places. "We'll be gentle."

Marty placed a small lantern in the center of the table and powered on the field recorder. "Levels," he said. "Harrison?"

"Check, one, two," my co-host droned in that maddeningly calm baritone. "Ambient wind, distant traffic, possible owl."

"Shaunie?"

"Hi, spooky friends," I said, smile audible because I've trained it to be. "We're here at Saint Benedict's Cemetery with Sage Hollow's own Medium Matchmaker, Esme, to talk about the stories the stones still tell."

"Hot," Marty said under his breath. Thanks to my perpetual enthusiasm, I got that critique a lot. "And Esme?"

"Welcome to the threshold," she murmured, and my skin did the goosebump thing it did for good music and bad decisions.

"Nearly there," Marty removed the headphones as he dug into his duffel, coming out with a camera. "Let's get some footage before we lose light."

We moved along a path the color of over-steeped tea,

with Marty walking backwards ahead of us, filming. I tucked my hands into my vest pockets and tried not to step on names. Harrison walked beside me, and every so often his knuckles brushed my sleeve, an accident that set off these tiny static pops under my skin. (I pretended it was just the polyester.)

"Any local legends we should cue up?" I asked Esme, keeping my voice soft. "Besides Archie, who babysits your shop."

She smiled as she looked out over the stones. "There's a story I like about a girl named Viola Bell who left home-made cookies on a fence post every Sunday for a boy she never married. He went to sea; she went to seasons. The post is still there." She gestured to a split-rail bit of fence at the edge, a spot worn smooth where human palms had lingered.

"Unrequited carbs," I said. "Tragic."

Harrison's mouth tugged upward, but he raced to cover it with a cough because heaven forbid he admit I was funny.

We circled back to our little table, just as the remnants of daylight gave way to the night sky. The crowd seemed to have multiplied, setting tiny bat babies loose in my stomach. I wasn't a stranger to being in the public eye, but I rarely recorded in front of a large audience. Even during the height of my vlogging days, most of the content I filmed was during private tours where the audience was minimal. Since shifting my focus to the podcast, most of the content that involved me speaking happened in a closed studio. It was better that way. Inevitably, I'd say something weird, or veer off course (or both), and have to be brought back by my co-host or my producer.

I found my seat on the long edge of the rectangular table beside Harrison who was checking the wind noise with his hand up like a priest blessing us with silence. Esme was on my other side, catty-corner, so she could easily speak to both of us. She sat with her palms open, the lantern light catching the river-rock bracelets on her wrists.

Marty, standing between us and the crowd, leaned over the table and whispered, "Ten minutes of chit chat, then we can try other instruments." He glanced at me. "Shaunie, not your crystals. The EMF."

"I was going to suggest a quartz pendulum," I whispered back, offended. I'd brought mine for the occasion.

We rolled. I did the host patter: where we were, who we were with, why Saint Benedict's. Harrison, glasses on, countered with a pocket history in his professor voice, which definitely wasn't doing weird things to my insides. Other girls, probably, but not me.

"Question," I said, when Marty circled a finger to cue a pivot. "Esme, you grew up here in Sage Hollow. You've heard the stories of local lore, so how do you tell if what you hear as a medium is memory or mind? If what you feel is a you thing or a there thing?" I pointed up toward the sky. Heaven. The Universe.

"The information they tell me is not a part of our history, oral or written," she replied. "Practice helps with clarity."

"Feel up for practice right now?"

"Yes, but first we need consent." She tipped her head toward the stones. "We always ask."

I nodded. "May we ask now?"

"You just did." She smiled and went very still.

It wasn't dramatic. No head tilt, no gasp, no eyes rolled white. Just Esme sitting under the old sugar maple with the lantern lighting her face like a study in candlelight. The breeze got curious, tugging at my beanie; the hair on my arms lifted like it had heard a song I couldn't.

"There's a woman near," Esme said softly. "Not tied here. She came with a visitor." Her gaze slid past me.

Harrison's posture didn't change as he gestured toward the crowd. "We're in a cemetery," he said, level. "Lots of women near."

Esme's smile bent, almost fond. "This one is very specific. Mother energy. She keeps showing me triangles." She paused. "Toast, I think. Yes, toast. With cinnamon and sugar." A longer pause. "She cut the crusts off when her son was sad."

I felt Harrison go very still, like a violin string pulled taut. The EMF meter on the table murmured once, a little green hiccup, followed by a collective gasp from the audience.

Marty's eyes went wide. He frantically mimed *keep rolling.*

Harrison, ever the skeptic, pushed, "Triangles is a common way to cut toast," he said, too mild, the way people talk when they're deciding whether to run.

Esme simply tilted her head, as if listening a little harder, and added, "She says, 'I didn't like the hospital coffee, but I loved how you brought me cinnamon sugar so it would taste like home.'"

My co-host swallowed, then covered his discomfort by adjusting in is chair. If Esme was to be believed, then she was channeling Harrison's mom who had passed away nine years ago. Harrison hadn't told me that, of course; the man was an oyster protecting a precious pearl at all times. I'd learned about her when I'd done my deep dive on the web after Marty had made him my counterpart on the show. I had needed to know what I was getting myself into, obviously. He hadn't had much of an online presence, but I'd stumbled upon an obituary for his mother who had lost a long battle with cancer, leaving behind her only son. He was twenty-one.

"We can stop," I said, voice low, pitched just for Harrison even though we were on mic. "We can stop."

He didn't look at me.

Esme, eyes closed, continued, "She says, 'I was not brave. You were.' She says...oh." Her expression softened. "She says, 'My angel.'"

Harrison made a sound, tiny and involuntary, like a hinge that hadn't been used in a while.

The noise punched the air out of the pocket behind my ribs.

His fingers clenched into a fist until his knuckles went pale.

I found my voice. "Harrison," I whispered, gentler than I normally know how to be on the first try. "We can cut. Say the word."

He cleared his throat. Twice. When he spoke, the dryness was back, the control. "Let's take a break."

Marty's producer-brain wanted to argue, but to his credit, he cut the recorder. "Five," he said briskly. "Hydrate. No wandering."

Harrison walked a little ways off toward a low wall where a carpet of leaves gathered. He didn't sit. Just stood, shoulders squared like a person presenting a target to a storm. I gave him space for twelve counts and then followed, because space is not the same thing as separation.

"I can tell her to dial it back," I said, toeing a pinecone. "Esme. She doesn't need to go there."

"Go where?" he asked, perfectly even. It would have been a good act if his jaw hadn't betrayed him by ticking.

"Where it hurts," I said. "On tape."

He huffed a laugh that didn't have humor in it, then glanced at me and something that wasn't skepticism moved through his eyes. He looked away before it could be anything dangerous. "She could have Googled," he said, because of course he would. It was so Harrison of him that I wanted to kiss his forehead and also strangle him a little.

"She could have," I agreed. "But I live online, and the cinnamon triangles aren't out there."

He didn't answer, but his dark eyes held mine for a beat. A silent understanding passed between us where he acknowledged that I was aware of his mother's demise.

Behind us, Marty did a soft clap, forcing us to disconnect. "We can pivot segments," he called, careful to keep it casual. "Do some general cemetery lore, get the EMF to go haywire, and call it. We have plenty."

Harrison exhaled. "Let's finish the segment. Briefly. No more of...that."

"Got it." Marty led the way back.

I wanted to reach for Harrison—wrist, sleeve, anything —but instead I reached for the thing I could fix and tucked a flyaway cable into his pocket, neat as a prayer.

We returned to the lantern's pool of light. Esme's face was calm, like a pond that had learned to keep secrets. "I'm sorry," she said to Harrison, quiet. "I don't go where I'm not invited but sometimes love finds a crack."

He nodded once. "Let's keep it general."

Marty tugged on his headphones and signaled for us to continue.

"There is another woman. Grandmother energy." Esme spun her head toward the crowd. "Italian. She says her granddaughter is here."

Several murmurs came from our audience.

"Hang on." Marty plucked a handheld out of our gear bag and got it set before signaling Esme to continue.

"I smell garlic and oil." She scanned the crowd. Once. Twice. Before pinpointing a petite woman with her stare. "May I give you a message?"

The auburn-haired woman nodded.

Marty extended the microphone and waved her closer.

"Your grandmother says, 'thank you for making my recipes for your family and keeping our traditions.'"

Tears welled up in the woman's eyes.

I could practically feel Harrison's skepticism and heard his voice in my head saying something like, *it's an obvious guess that an Italian grandmother liked to cook and has family recipes.*

I nearly shushed him.

Esme turned her palm, fingers up, almost like some kind of flower. She then began to mime peeling back the petals. "What is this?" It was unclear who she was speaking to— living or...not living. "An artichoke. Does that make sense?"

The woman cracked a smile, filled with emotion. "Yes. Her stuffed artichokes are a tradition."

"Ah. You have a daughter?" Esme asked.

"Yes." She pointed to a young girl standing in front of a tall, muscular man. The father, I presumed.

"She says, 'I sent them to you. I knew you would feel it when you met him.' She means your husband. And something about fate. Does that make sense to you?"

The woman nodded furiously.

"You're here on vacation?"

"We are."

"Your grandmother keeps saying, 'Autumn.' This must be your favorite season."

Her jaw hung slack for a moment before she could find

her words. "It is my favorite season, but also, my name is Autumn."

The audience's shock would make for an excellent soundbite. My hand landed on Harrison's shoulder and shook him with excitement, which probably annoyed the grouch, but I didn't dare tear my attention away from what was unfolding to check. Annoyed was his default around me, so it was a safe bet.

"Ah. Then the D and the M initials must be your husband and daughter."

"Dylan and Maddie," the woman confirmed.

This time I couldn't contain my enthusiasm. "You're incredible, Esme."

She placed a hand over her heart. "I am merely a vessel. Spirit does the work, and I listen."

"Autumn, what is going through your head right now?" I asked.

"I don't know that I can put it in words."

That was problematic for our podcast. By nature, we relied on words. I pivoted. "You mentioned you are here on vacation. Where from?"

"Manhattan."

"A Yankee in Patriot country." That earned me a laugh.

"What brought you to Sage Hollow, NH?" Harrison interjected, which was probably a good thing because I was fairly certain I'd mixed up my sports.

"Well, my husband is a fireman in the FDNY, and one of the guys he works with recommended we bring our daughter here for the Harvest Festival. He said there was no better place to spend Halloween."

"Halloween capital." Esme gave Harrison a told-you-so look, which I loved on account of it usually being me on the receiving end of his version of that expression.

We wound down the interview with the tourist, then moved on. We did history. We did respectful spook. We did three minutes on folk beliefs around cider and graveyards because apparently that's a thing (offering apples to the dead in harvest months, who knew?). The EMF stayed mostly quiet save for a few spikes. A barn owl startled us all by ghosting from the sugar maple and Harrison didn't swear into the mic, which I considered an act of God.

FIVE

When Marty gave the cut motion, the wind swung the iron gate, and it squealed like an out of tune cello. "Hot chocolate?" Marty asked as he wound a cable. "On me. I saw a cart with whipped cream like a cumulus cloud."

As I slung Winnie onto my back, my mouth curved because I'm helpless against sugar. "Yes. Please."

Esme touched my sleeve. Her hand was warm the way fresh bread is. "May I walk with you for a moment, Siobhan?"

"Of course." I glanced at Harrison.

"Meet you at the gate," he said without looking up, which meant *I need sixty seconds where my face can do private things.*

I nodded.

Esme and I strolled a short distance along the fence toward Viola Bell's unrequited love post, and my feet took over, giving me no choice but to keep going so I could touch it.

"Your partner is what we call a skeptic, no?"

I kicked at the dirt with the toe of my boot, not wanting

to lie, but also not wanting to insult her. "You could say that."

"I hope I did not cross a boundary by channeling his mother," Esme said, not as an apology; more like a weather report. "She was very insistent."

I glanced over my shoulder at Harrison who was shoulder-to-shoulder with Marty, hovering over a camera. "She called him her angel." My voice did the wobble I hate. "I can't decide if that's adorable or if I want to lie down on the ground and cry about it."

"Both things can be true. He is in a hard place. Not because of me."

I leaned against the cookie post. "Does she, I mean, does she want something from him? Or for him?"

"For," Esme replied immediately. "Always for. She keeps showing me a cedar box." She tapped two fingers lightly over her heart. "Something he thinks he's keeping safe by not opening."

I thought of the way Harrison tidied his emotions into neat stacks and labeled them *later*. "Okay." I thought of the EMF meter's little green gasp and my mouth got dry. "Okay."

Esme squeezed my hand once, then let go. "Hot chocolate," she suggested softly. "And laughter. The living have their rituals, too."

We rejoined the boys at the gate. Harrison met my eyes just long enough to nod, then fell into step beside me, not too close, but also not far, like magnets who hadn't decided if they were opposed or aligned. A little white feather poking through a seam on his puffy jacket caught my eye. Before I could stop myself, I reached for his arm and plucked it out and held it up for him to see. "Your angels want your attention."

He shrugged.

The hot-chocolate cart did in fact whip cream into weather systems. The vendor wore a scarf that could qualify as a blanket and had cinnamon sticks tucked in a jar like wands. No surprise, I ordered the pumpkin spice-flavored one with extra nutmeg, while Harrison took his without whipped cream because he is an affront to joy.

"Tomorrow is a free day until five o'clock when we have to set up for Shaunie's date," Marty said casually while we cradled our cups against our chins to fend off the early-evening chill. "We'll keep gear minimal. Very reality show. The camera will be there without being there."

"Copy," I said, trying to sound like a person who was not mentally spiraling about a kiss with a man I hadn't met yet while standing next to a different man whose shadows had me wrapped up like tangled Christmas tree lights.

Winnie, who had been politely pretending to be asleep in her carrier, stuck one paw through a hole on the side like *I would also like some cocoa.*

"Absolutely not," Harrison told her, which made me laugh harder than it deserved.

After saying goodbye to Esme and thanking her again, we drifted back toward the inn.

"I've heard some nights you can see the ghost of the original innkeeper right there." I pointed toward the first-floor window under the covered porch.

Marty advanced up the steps. "The haunted inn tour is the day after tomorrow."

Harrison, being Harrison, said nothing, but I caught the eye roll I swear he reserved just for me.

Inside, the scent of clove oil and lemon polish told us Betty had been crusading against dust. We left Marty, so he could do whatever it was he did to keep us relevant on the internet, and continued up to the honeymoon suite. While we were gone, my bed had been made up, Harrison's blanket had been folded and stacked with his pillow, and the room divider had been returned to its resting place against the wall.

Harrison removed his jacket, set his bag down on the chaise, then stood with his hands on the back of it like he wasn't sure what to do if they weren't busy. "About earlier," he said, eyes fixed on a point approximately two inches to the left of my shoulder.

I turned, half expecting to see Mildred peeking through a beaded curtain.

"What are you looking at?" he asked, his voice devoid of the annoyance I'd expected.

"At what you're looking at."

"I'm looking at you."

"Now you are, but you weren't a few seconds ago." I placed Winnie's carrier on the bed and unzipped it. "Be free." She hopped out, stretched each of her legs, then disappeared to the bathroom to take care of her kitty business.

"What was I looking at then?"

I gestured behind me. "Something over there."

"No, I really wasn't," Harrison insisted.

"You just really like the wallpaper, then, huh?"

"What are you...?" He shook his head and pinched the bridge of his nose. "As I was saying, or trying to—"

"Sorry," I blurted as I plopped onto the foot of the bed, its springs letting out a squeak, which was very unfortunate being that this was a *honeymoon* suite. A memory foam mattress would've been a smarter choice.

"For what?"

"Interrupting you." I removed my outer layers and laid them on the dust cover.

"I'm used to you by now."

I tucked my legs underneath me, criss-cross applesauce. "It was rude of me. I didn't mean to, but my brain..." I trailed, letting him fill in the blank.

He released his death grip on the chaise (I'm sure the frilly fabric was grateful it could breathe again) and took two and a half steps toward me. The half is because he stopped mid-stride and rocked back; almost as if he was going to come sit with me or something, then thought better of it. *Interesting...*

He slid his hands into his front pockets. "How many times do I have to tell you not to apologize for the way you are before you'll stop?"

I shrugged a shoulder. After a lifetime of having others be frustrated with me, apologizing had become my default. It drove my parents mad when I failed to focus, and my ex-boyfriend *hated* when I interrupted him. I tugged off my pumpkin beanie and smoothed my hands over my hair. "But I am sorry."

"Siobhan," his voice dipped into a lower octave, commanding my attention, yet possessing a tenderness that wasn't present in his usual dry tone. "Your ADHD isn't a flaw, it's your operating system."

I hummed as I considered that for a moment.

When I didn't respond, he inched one step closer. "It's part of your brilliance."

My eyes went wide. "Was that a compliment, Harry?"

Winnie emerged from the bathroom, crossed between us and hopped up onto the bed, dispersing the weird static that'd been sparking in the air."

"Don't let it get to your head." He turned, claimed some

distance, and unzipped his bag. "What I was trying to say...about that interview—"

"We won't use it without your permission. Not even a breath."

The tension in his shoulders loosened by a molecule. "Thank you."

"We can put the footage in a little cedar box and lock it away," I said before my mouth could check with my brain.

He looked over his shoulder at me, startled enough that I felt it, which was a weird thing to feel from a look. "What?"

"Nothing," I said too fast. "Just brain static. Ignore me."

He didn't push, which I will be grateful for once I stopped wanting to crawl under the bed. Instead, he clicked his pen. "I'm going to dump cards and label tracks. Then, I might take a walk."

"Bring a scarf," I said, because that is how I say *don't be alone with heavy things longer than you have to.* "It's colder after dark."

He nodded. The corner of his mouth did that almost-smile that made me feel like I'd won a prize I shouldn't want. "Statistically likely," he replied, donning his drab personality like armor, and then we were both saved by the radiator clearing its throat, reminiscent of an old actor about to deliver a Shakespearean monologue.

While he worked, I cleaned up our clutter (fine, *my* clutter), folded Switzerland the Room Divider back into place, and put my smoky quartz on the mantel like a sentry. Winnie made biscuits on the throw pillow with an almost religious fervor.

My phone buzzed with a text from an unknown number.

Unknown: Hey Shaunie. Dalton here. Hope it's cool my mom gave me your number. Looking forward to meeting you tomorrow. I'll bring Patch. He's a gentleman. Most of the time.

A second message appeared before I could process the first.

Unknown: Also, if you need a drink before six, stop by the pumpkin patch at the Harvest Festival. Cider's on me. (And yes, I know that's a bribe. Guilty.)

I stared at the little bubbles like they were tarot cards. *Think of something clever.* I came up with great lines for my show all the time, surely, I could come up with something flirty—but not too flirty—to say in response. It's not like I'd never dated or been hit on before.

Somewhere to my left, a pen clicked, two beats, then one (Harrison's rhythm when he's labeling). Fleeting, the idea of asking him what I should say came and went. We weren't the kind of friends who gave each other dating advice. Heck, I wasn't even sure we were the kind of friends who were...friends.

I spun on my heels to face the desk with a hand on my hip. "Are we friends?"

"Excuse me?" He peered over the frame of his glasses.

My nose wrinkled. I really needed to work on my filter because not all my thoughts were meant to be outside thoughts. Too far down the rabbit hole to scramble out, I repeated, "Are we friends. You and me?"

"Uhhh..."

"I know we're not like friends-friends, but are we *friends?*" My hand (the one not on my hip) overly gesticulated like it was in a solo game of charades, making my bangles jingle an out of rhythm tune.

"I don't understand the question."

My body bent in half at the waist with a harumph. "C'mon, Harry. Use all those smarts you've got and figure it out."

The corner of his mouth twitched, but he cleared his throat and returned to neutral (which, in his case, was stoicism). "Well, statistically—"

"No statistics." I groaned. "Do I need to write it out for you?" I stomped over to the desk, plucked up a pen, tore a slip of paper out from under his laptop, knocking a few things out of place in the process, and scribbled:

Are we friends? Circle one.
Yes
No

While he was busy reorienting his discs to whatever degree angle he insisted they be at that evening, I tossed the pen on the desk and thrust the note at him.

His dark eyes dipped to the paper, then up at me, then down to the paper. Neither one of us said a thing, but my heavy breathing filled the silence. What felt like an hour later, Harrison did his best impression of a sloth as he reached for the pen and slipped the note from my sweaty hand.

Too nervous to watch, I occupied my eyes by counting the number of cinnamon-scented branches in the vase on the end table near the chaise. It was a really difficult task to do from that distance, and I had to keep starting over. The click of the ballpoint tip retracting into the cylinder made me turn. Harrison had folded the paper in half and was holding it out for me.

As nonchalantly as possible (which, for me, wasn't very), I took it, unfolded it and frowned when I didn't see a circle. Instead, his stupidly neat handwriting filled the space beneath mine.

Do you want to be friends? Circle one.
Yes.
No.

"Who puts periods after *yes* and *no*?" I asked because, of course, I would.

"They are complete sentences."

"But they're in a list."

"Still sentences."

"You know what?" I crumpled the note into a ball. "Never mind." Spinning on my heels, I stomped toward the room divider and dragged it (not an easy feat because it did little hops on the carpet) until it blocked my view of the desk from my bed, then I collapsed beside Winnie.

After feeling around the comforter until I found my phone, I opened my messages and, before I could overthink things further, typed:

Hi Dalton! Looking forward to it. I'm bribable, FYI. Especially by cider. See you at six.

Through the screen, Harrison said my name like he'd been practicing not to. "Siobhan?"

"Yeah?"

He hesitated, then, said, "We can be friends."

After a few heartbeats, I replied softly, "Okay."

The suite settled around us, old house noises mimicked Winnie shifting in her sleep. Somewhere outside, a dog barked—far, eager. Maybe it was Patch testing his voice against the darkness. I stared at the ceiling until the stucco pattern swam. Somewhere in the walls, the pipes murmured to each other in a language I almost understood.

Possibly it said: *One kiss.*

Possibly it said: *Be careful with what you think you want.*

Possibly it just said: *Mildred needs a raise.*

I closed my eyes and tried not to imagine the shape of a mouth I hadn't met yet compared to the one across the room.

SIX

Our so-called "free day" wasn't exactly free. Marty had us gathering what he called "texture" (translation: me pointing at things and saying, "Spooky," while Harrison filmed them like a nature documentarian), but he kept us un-mic'd and relatively unbothered. Plus, I looked too cute that day to *not* film. Under my dark-wash denim overalls I wore a white turtleneck with horizontal black pinstripes, and tied around my waist was an orange, knit sweater. I accessorized with glossy black, chunky-heeled boots and a black, velvet fedora that had an orange and brown feather tucked into the leather band. My hair was done in a loose side-braid that had pink wisps poking out of it. Some people balked at the combination of pink and orange, but I happened to love it.

In the afternoon, Harrison and I were permitted to go to the fairgrounds where the main festival was held so I could film some BTS for my vlog and socials, but we were relegated to the area immediately inside the entrance. Marty wanted the full fair experience to happen on a date with Dalton, assuming there would be a second date. I believe his exact words were, "Fairs are romantic. Very Noah and Allie.

The setting screams virality." I'd agreed to go along with it but drew the line at making Dalton climb up the outside of a Ferris wheel.

From what we saw of it, there was a pumpkin wall big enough to qualify as a fortress, a face-painter turning toddlers into tigers, a brass trio playing something jaunty near a blacksmithing demonstration. The hammering of metal on metal was practically the band's fourth member. I bought a caramel apple I did not need and ate it anyway while Harrison pretended he wasn't keeping an eye on how sticky my hands were getting near the camera lenses.

"Wipes," he said, handing me a packet like a dad at a playground.

"Bossy," I said, taking them, which is how I say *thank you* without giving him the satisfaction.

He was back in practical uniform—dark flannel, nerd tee (*Legends of the Hidden Temple*), and the kind of watch that looked like it had opinions it would gladly share if you stood close to it for too long. If you didn't know him, you'd think he was all edges. I knew better. Some of his parts were soft—he just stored them in a cedar box.

Once we had some solid footage, and I was thoroughly de-stickified, it was time to return so I could get ready for my date. We approached a volunteer in a blaze-orange vest who flagged down one of the complimentary golf carts that zipped people between the fairgrounds and Middle Hollow Road. Our driver, a woman with a gray braid, pumpkin earrings, and a name tag that said *Dot*, thumbed over her shoulder. "Hop on, podcast people. I promise not to dump you in the corn maze."

"After you," Harrison said, like a gentleman, and then he climbed in beside me. His knees knocked mine, and I held Winnie's backpack firmly on my lap, as Dot peeled away with the confidence of a retired stunt driver. Dot pointed two fingers at her eyes and then at us in the rearview. "No canoodling. This is a family vehicle."

"We professionally annoy each other. Closest we get," I assured.

"Adorable," Dot said, deadpan, before taking a corner like she was qualifying for Daytona.

Harrison braced a hand on the seat in front of us. Once we were on a straightaway, he put on his glasses, then pulled his phone out of his pocket. "Okay. Here's the plan," he said, opening a notes doc titled, *Dalton Date: Boundaries/Questions*.

I groaned for show and leaned back, wind teasing the ends of my hair. "Hit me, coach."

"Ground rules first. One: You don't have to answer anything you don't want to. If you want out, left earlobe."

"What about my earlobe?"

"Touch it."

"I refuse to flirt with my earlobe in public," I said, but my hand did a test brush anyway.

Clearly choosing to ignore me, he continued, "Two: No prophecy talk unless he brings it up."

"Rude to fate." I feigned offense. But also, if I couldn't talk about the prophecy, what the heck should I talk about? The night before, when "the plumbing," as Harrison had insisted, had woken me up, I'd stayed awake crafting an entire conversation in my head revolving around the mysterious Esme and what her prediction could mean. I had enough content to fill an entire hour's podcast interview. "Oh!" I exclaimed, craning my neck to peer around him. "Did you see that kid's witch hat? I wonder if she got it at the fair. I need one. It's giving Glinda meets Sally Skellington. Wouldn't I look good—"

"Three: No promises you don't want our audience holding you to. No 'we'll do this every year' or 'we'll name our first puppy Patch Junior' on mic."

As though she understood him, because of course she did, Winnie hissed—the low, rumble of a displeased fire-breathing dragon issuing a warning. *I feel you, sister.* Not that there was anything wrong with dogs, but cats are clearly the superior of the two. Dogs are cute. Cats are majestic. Actually, I'd bet Winnie would love to be called, Your Majesty. That gave me a costume idea for her, and I made a mental note to search for the nearest pet supply and craft stores because she would look so stinking cute with a robe, scepter, and crown. I already had a costume for her to wear on Halloween, but she—

"Shaunie," Harrison said, recalling my attention.

"What?" *Oh, yeah.* "Fine. I'll keep my Patch Junior aspirations private," I replied before leaning down and whispering to my baby, "Don't worry. I would never replace you with a dog." Her weight shifted on my lap as she settled into a relaxed curl.

"Four: If he asks to go off the record, we stop. Marty will live."

The cart lurched as Dot gear-shifted us in traffic up the hill toward town.

Harrison swiped his screen. "For questions, softballs first. 'What do you love most about Sage Hollow in Harvest Week?'"

"Acceptable. I can talk fall fanfare and PSLs like they constitute a religion."

He snorted. "I am aware. Next, 'Perfect autumn day. Describe it.'"

"Apple picking. Pumpkin carving. Leaf pile jumping. Me not getting murdered by one of the Inn's ghosts."

Dot gave me a thumbs-up. "Put that on a tote bag."

"You're asking him these questions. Our audience already knows *your* answer. Next. 'What's something you wish people understood about small-town businesses?'" Harrison went on and on. "'What's Patch's job description at the pumpkin patch?'"

"Greeter, therapist, union rep," I said. "He does tricks for treats. See what I did there?"

"Hey, that's good. You're a funny one," Dot said with a laugh. At least someone in the vehicle found me humorous.

Mr. Stick-in-the-Mud continued, "Again, when you ask these questions, don't also provide his answer for him."

"Right. Sorry. It's just I had a good answer for that one."

His eyes locked on me as if to say, *what'd I tell you about apologizing?* And the intensity nearly had me saying sorry a second time, but I refrained. Instead, I squirmed, making the vinyl seat squeak against my denim overalls. "Next question," I whispered.

His attention returned to his phone. "'What's your favorite memory at your family's orchard that doesn't involve a camera?'" He glanced at me over his glasses. "That one screens for performative answers."

"Look at you, Dr. Phil."

He ignored me. "Potential land mines, we approach gently. 'Your mom, Lynnette, is enthusiastic and proactive. How does her playing matchmaker land for you?' If he stiffens, we pivot."

"Don't you dare make me say 'boundaries with mom' on a first date," I warned.

"That's important. She's a bit of a red flag."

"How do you figure? She was perfectly nice."

"What you call nice, I call desperate for her five minutes of fame."

We rattled onto Middle Hollow Road beneath the festival banner, and the sugar maples along the sidewalk rustled like they were passing notes.

"Two values questions," he said. "'What does your ideal day look like when no one is watching?' and 'When the festival's over and the town goes quiet, what do you keep doing anyway?'"

"Those are wicked good."

"I know," he said, like I'd complimented a spreadsheet, which was Harrison for *thank you*.

Dot slowed for a family crossing with cider, then gunned it again. "You kids sound prepared."

"He is most definitely not a kid. But I'm still a kid at heart. At least fifty percent of me is gummy bears. But only the green and red ones. The others are sour." I stuck out my tongue.

"Let me guess. You're interviewing Dalton. Am I right?" Dot braked in the line of traffic.

I stuck my finger through one of the holes in Winnie's bag and gave her a scratch. "Correct. Except it's not an interview, it's a date."

"Really?"

Harrison cleared his throat. "Moving on. 'What does *listening* mean to you?' 'When something awkward happens, do you default to jokes, honesty, or do you vanish into your corn maze?' And 'What's your relationship to attention? Do you like it, hate it, tolerate it?'"

"Should I also ask his feelings on haunted dolls, or is that third date material?"

"Third," he said, completely serious. "Tonight stays light."

If that list was Harrison's idea of light, it was no wonder he was still single.

"Lastly, if he asks you anything you don't want in the episode, you have full veto. I will back your play."

Warmth slid under my sternum, surprising and a little dangerous. I covered it with sarcasm like a sensible coat. "So protective. Is this because you fear for your precious audio levels if I cry?"

"It's because you're not content," he said without looking at me. "You're my co-ho... friend."

Dot cut him a look in the rearview that said *mmhmm*. My mouth went soft, which I hid by covering it with my braid.

The golf cart bounced over a seam in the road. "End of the line," Dot announced.

"Thanks for the ride," I said as I climbed down and slung Winnie over my shoulder. "Any last wisdom to share?"

"Drink water, trust your gut, and don't treat a date like an interview, podcast girl." She ticked them off on her ringed fingers, then sped away from the curb.

Harrison pocketed his phone as we made our way up the stone path. "I'll email the list so you have it."

"Thanks, Harry."

We climbed the steps, then he reached for the door and held it, while I pretended that the gentlemanly gesture was no big deal—like Winnie would. She never made a fuss over me when I fed her, or brushed her, or carried her around, or cleaned up her poop. *Queens don't fuss*, I could practically hear her say.

"One last thing," he said as we crossed the threshold and were assaulted with the sweet scent of cinnamon. "You don't owe us a *moment*. Not Marty, not our listeners, not this town."

Unable to help myself, because...no filter, I asked, "What about you?"

"Especially not me. I've been against this from the beginning.

"Then why make that list?" I paused at the bottom of the staircase.

"Because preparing is what I do." That was true. For our episodes, I was more of a wing-it kind of girl, whereas he always showed up with copious notes. "And for some reason you're dead set on following this plan."

"Umm, hello? Were you not there when Esme told me I only have a few days to have a life-changing kiss? This is my only prospect. Of course. I'm following this plan."

"You'd better get ready then." Some sort of emotion flashed behind his eyes, but I couldn't quite place it. "I'm going to meet with Marty. Give you space." He turned and left through the door we had just entered.

"What was that about?" I asked Winnie.

Her meowed reply sounded an awful lot like she didn't know either.

BY FOUR-THIRTY, I'd cycled through six outfit options, panicked, and landed on the first one again: a black sweater dress, tights, boots, a fuzzy orange jacket that evoked pumpkin chic. The whole look was giving *Buffy the Vampire Slayer* goes for coffee. I tucked a rose quartz into my bra and, because I am me, slipped on dangly pumpkin earrings. Winnie judged me from the bed with the resigned air of a cat who has seen too much.

"Don't look at me in that tone," I told her. "Some of us have a prophecy to live up to. Don't you want a daddy?"

She blinked, unimpressed, and began licking a paw.

Same, girl.

Fifteen minutes later, we convened in the inn's foyer. Marty wore his "I'm pretending to be chill even though I'm jumping out of my skin with excitement" grin and Harrison carried a tense-jawed expression I couldn't read. They each carried a gear bag. *So much for minimal equipment.*

As we made the short walk to the cafe, Harrison said, "Ground rules," as if we hadn't already discussed them. "If you want out, touch your left earlobe."

Marty clapped once. "Let it be whatever it is," he reminded us, which is producer for *if it's a disaster, fantastic.*

Black Cat Coffee Co.'s patio had strung orange bulbs like beads and set out plaid blankets as if the air needed help being cozy. The bell gave its proud *clonk* as we came through. The girl with the bat-wing eyeliner was there again, and she guided us to a corner table outside near a heater that made a polite shhh.

While I settled into the chair with Winnie, trying my best to conceal my pounding heart, the guys set up lights and tripods and taped down cord after cord after cord. That corner of the patio had been roped off for us, and some of the other customers eyed us with curiosity. No doubt they were trying to figure out if we were filming an episode of *The Real Housewives of New Hampshire.*

I scoffed. *As if.* Like I could ever be a housewife.

"What?" Harrison, who was on all fours under the table, glanced up from his roll of duct tape.

"What, what?" I asked, genuinely confused.

"You made a noise?"

"I did?"

He nodded.

"What kind of noise?"

"Like this." He blew air out his nose.

"Oh." I wrapped my arms around Winnie's carrier.

He tilted his head. "You good?"

"Great," I lied. "Sorry, I was having an internal conversation with myself."

He crawled out, stood, leaned close to my ear, and whispered in a low rasp, "I thought we had an agreement about that word."

That sound should not have woken the bats in my gut-cave, but it did. I swallowed. "Sor— I mean...never mind."

Without another word, he returned to work like he hadn't just made me forget how to breathe. There'd been way too many occurrences during that trip where he'd flipped the switch from nerdy Harrison to sneaky-hot Harry, and I didn't know what to do with that.

Marty approached, placed my body pack on the table, and held out his hands. "Give me Winnie."

I pouted and held the carrier tighter. "Why?"

"Because we don't know how Patch is with cats, and we already know how Win feels about dogs. Remember the incident at that haunted junkyard last spring?"

I shuddered as I recalled how the three Rottweilers had chased after Marty while he ran around the property holding Winnie and hollering at the yard's owner to call off his hounds. "But Dalton can't be my soulmate if our fur-babies hate each other. It's better to find out now before we get too invested."

Marty clasped his hands together in front of his chest, and I braced myself for a dad lecture. "Shaunie, I appreciate your commitment to the bit, but that's what this is, okay? Don't hang your future on a psychic prediction and a pumpkin farmer."

I fiddled with my rings and narrowed my eyes, assessing. Marty wasn't a skeptic, per se, but he wasn't a full believer either. He was in the entertainment business, and our show...well...it was entertaining but, surely, he couldn't think Esme's prophecy was some hoax. "You sound like Harrison."

He checked his watch and let out a sigh. "Can I please have Winnie? They'll be here any minute and you need to mic up." His tone was gentle, even though I knew he was growing impatient.

My grip didn't loosen.

Marty shook his head in defeat, then went over to Harrison. While the two talked out of earshot, I slipped a finger into the bag and pet my girl. When they split apart, our producer went inside, and Harrison approached my table.

"I need to check your levels." He nudged the pack toward me. "Marty went out front to get Dalton set up. He wants to catch the initial meeting on camera."

I gasped. "He's here already?"

"I don't know. I'm with you."

My palms grew clammy, so I tried to dry them on my coat, but the synthetic fur simply stuck to my hands. "Oh my God, now I look like a character from *Sesame Street*." I held them up for Harrison to see.

He offered me his arm. "Here."

I glanced between him, and his flannel covered forearm. "Here, what?"

"Use my sleeve."

I cocked my head. "Really?"

He moved closer.

Tentatively, I reached out but stopped short of touching him. "Why are you being so nice?"

"I'm always nice."

"You're mostly grumpy."

The hint of a chuckle escaped his lips. "And you're always honest."

"Is that a bad thing?" I asked, my hands still hovering just above his arm.

"No. It's appreciated. Come on. My offer expires."

I ran my hands over his forearms, and they glided over a ridge, then dipped. It felt kind of good, so I did it again. There was something weirdly sensual about the hardness of his muscle beneath the soft flannel.

"Umm, I think, maybe, you're all set?"

I released him like a burning log, and my cheeks flushed, embarrassed that I'd turned his kind gesture into an opportunity to feel him up. "Right. Sorry." I cringed. "Shoot. Sorry." I groaned at my inability to control the connection between my brain and my mouth.

"It's fine." He picked up my pack and handed it to me.

An owl hooted in the distance. "Did you hear that?" I asked. It seemed a bit early in the night to be hearing owls. But what did I know? I lived in a city where the most exotic nature we encountered was a black squirrel.

"Yeah."

I wondered if it was the same one we'd seen at the cemetery as I moved Winnie onto the table, then removed my coat.

Harrison scooped up the carrier and swung it over his shoulder.

"Hey!" I stood and grabbed for my cat, who was hissing something fierce, but he spun around, keeping her out of reach. "Give her back," I demanded.

"No." His voice was calm, dry.

"No?"

"I'm with Marty on this. Having a dog and a cat on camera in this confined space is statistically imprudent."

"Well, I think it's statistically *prudent* for me to have my emotional support cat when I need emotional support." Not wanting to admit he was right, I planted my hands on my hips and scowled.

"You want this to go well, don't you?"

"Of course."

"Then let me have her. I will be right over there." He pointed to a table in the corner where his laptop and audio interface sat. "I'll even wear the bag and turn around every so often for you to see her." He slipped his arms through the straps. Well, he tried to. They weren't loose enough.

That made me smile, and I cursed my mouth for doing me dirty like that. Harrison knew he'd won, so I conceded. "Fine, but you'd better."

He drew an X over his heart.

I'd barely gotten settled again after my sound check when a golden retriever bounded across the patio like a sunbeam with legs.

"Patch!" I squeaked, because manners. He sat beside me and lifted one paw like he was either greeting me or asking for the Wi-Fi password.

"Show-off," a voice said, as warm and sweet as cider.

I looked up into a face that appeared capable of selling pumpkins to the Grinch on Easter. Dalton Wakefield wore a hunter-green, quilted vest over a gray henley, and jeans with work boots. His hands were nicked in a way that said, *I fix things.* His fawn-brown hair did that good-boy swoop, and his smile...did the rest.

"Hi," I said, entirely too breathy as I stood and held out my hand just as he was leaning in for a hug. We did this awkward dance where he leaned away as I leaned forward, then back again. He laughed, stopping me just short of a panic attack, and pulled me to him for a quick hug.

After we broke apart, I tucked my hair behind my ear, and said, "Sorry about that. I'm Siobhan, but everyone just calls me Shaunie because—"

"Cut," Harrison called from behind his table.

Marty threw up his hands in exasperation. "I thought the levels were set."

Ignoring our producer, he tenderly placed Winnie's carrier on his table, making sure she faced away from the big, bag, golden retriever, then he approached. Turning his back to Dalton, he got between me and my date and took enough steps forward that I was forced to back up a couple of feet.

I gritted through my teeth, "If you're about to yell at me for saying sorry—"

"What? No," he whispered low enough so the others wouldn't hear. "Although, you should not have apologized to him. I cut because you touched your left ear."

My shoulders drooped. "I did?"

"Yeah."

"Oh. Oopsie." I gave him an apologetic grin.

"So, you weren't signaling me for help?"

I shook my head.

He nodded almost imperceptibly, then scurried toward his station, and donned Winnie like a scuba tank. "Continue."

"Now we have to run it again," Marty grumbled. "From the hug." He put his headphones back on.

Confusion was written all over Dalton's pretty, bearded face as his cornflower-blue eyes darted from me to my team.

"That's Harrison and Marty," I said. "It's best if you pretend they don't exist."

"Umm, sure. Alright."

Marty gave an exaggerated glance to the middle

distance while Harrison eyed a propane heater like it had profound thoughts.

"Let's start over." I was grateful for a second chance at my first impression. This time, I went straight in for a hug. "I'm Shaunie."

"Dalton," he returned. "And that upstager is Patch. We're both glad to meet you."

The dog thumped his tail in agreement.

We took our seats across from each other, with Patch lying between us, his chin on my boot. I took that as a good sign. Bat-wing (I really should've gotten her name) approached with our drinks, which Marty had ordered in advance to minimize interruptions. Dalton got a maple latte, decaf, because it was too late in the day for him to have caffeine. Apparently, farm life started before the sun. As someone allergic to mornings, I could never with a capital N.

PSL for me (shocker, I know), caffeinated, since I was practically immune. Even Patch got a pup cup treat, which he approached with the reverence of a pilgrim reaching a shrine. That made me think about hiking the El Camino one day. (Bucket list!) There were tons of spooky old buildings for me to investigate along the way. Plus, I'd never stayed in a hostel, and I'd heard—

"So," Dalton said, reminding me I was on a date. "Did my mom steamroll you into this, or are you voluntarily participating in the Wakefield family weirdness?"

"I'm voluntarily letting your mother be adorable," I replied, while trying to remember the question Harrison had told me to ask that would reveal whether Lynnette was a red flag. I turned toward my co-host/friend/roomie, and true to his word, he stood and spun around so I could see

Little Miss Winifred, who was soundly asleep. It made me smile.

"Thanks for being cool about it." Dalton drew me back in. "My mother regularly collects strangers and forces them to be friends. A lot of the residents here are like that. Small-town living and all. I apologize on the town's behalf."

I stole a sideways glance at Harrison to see if he got upset when other people said sorry, too, but if he did, he wasn't showing it.

After searching my memory for another question from the approved list, I came out with, "What's it like working here during the Harvest Festival?"

His mouth tipped. "We train all year for this. Apple picking is a contact sport. The pumpkin patch is where I go to repent."

"Repent for what?"

"Underestimating how personal people take apple-cider donuts."

"We are a donut-forward culture," I agreed. "One must never joke about the apple cider variety."

He let out a belly laugh. "You're hilarious."

My hand came up to tuck my hair behind my ear again, but I remembered at the last second and stopped, leaving my fingers to dangle awkwardly beside my cheek. My solution? Weave them through my hair and toss it dramatically to the other side.

That earned me another laugh.

I picked up my paper cup and took a soul-satisfying sip of the sweet autumn goodness.

Dalton told me about the press they set up for fresh cider, the line for hayrides, the teenagers who sneak into the corn maze to make out and think no one knows. I told him about the studio in Boston and the way Harrison alphabetizes *everything.* Dalton nodded in the right places, and he didn't interrupt. On paper, he was exactly what my mother would refer to as *steady,* which was listed at the top of her list of qualities I needed in a husband because someone had to balance my chaos.

"To be honest," he said, a little shy. "I've been a fan for a while. I've watched most, if not all, of your YouTube videos."

"You and a few hundred thousand of my closest friends," I muttered under my breath. Then, I scrunched my face because I was afraid to use my hands and risk being awkward again.

"What'd you say?" he asked.

"Which video is your favorite?" That was my go-to response when meeting fans.

He scratched at the hair covering his chin. "Probably the one where you went to the cacao ceremony on that ranch in Arizona."

I nodded, remembering it fondly.

Patch, who had whipped cream on his nose, sneezed theatrically. I wiped it off with a napkin and he gazed at me as if I'd awarded him a medal.

Dalton went on to sing my praises, which made me squirm in my chair. When I couldn't handle any more talk about me, I blurted out, "What's your favorite kitchen utensil?" Where that came from, I couldn't tell you, but it seemed a good a question as any.

Dalton hummed, but didn't take long before replying, "Whisk."

"That was fast. You have a whisk agenda?" *That was dumb.* I laughed because it was better to laugh at myself than wait for someone else to decide I was the joke.

He chuckled with me. "It's efficient and adaptable."

"You just described Harrison," I said, then wanted to take it back. Then didn't know why I wanted to take it back. Then I sipped my PSL to shut my mouth.

Dalton followed my accidental glance to the side table where Harrison was glued to his laptop. He looked down, gave Patch's ear a thoughtful rub, then said, "You two have good rhythm."

"Thank you. We annoy each other professionally," I replied, aiming for airy and landing closer to defensive. "It's our brand."

"Sure."

Moving on, I asked him to tell me more about his life in Sage Hollow while I scooted my legs closer to the heater. In retrospect, tights and a sweater dress weren't the best choice for an evening outdoor date in New Hampshire at the end of October.

Dalton explained that he handled the orchard's day-to-day operations with his uncle and kept an off-season workshop where he restored old wooden sleds for fun because, apparently, he was a character from a Hallmark movie. The tension dissipated as conversation flowed more naturally. Maybe that was the prophecy's trick: not fireworks, but a pilot light you didn't notice until everything warmed.

Marty did a tiny circle in the air—the *wrap soon* signal. I didn't want to leave yet, but I also didn't want to stay so long that we lapped ourselves.

Dalton leaned forward, elbows on the table. "Can I tell you something that might be weird?"

"That's my preferred genre."

"I know this all happened because of Esme, well, and my mom, but I don't want to see you to fulfill some prophecy. I'd like to ask you on a second date simply because the first one was good."

My mouth did a soft open like it was new to the concept of being asked out. "I would like that."

"Are you free tomorrow?"

"I can be."

"Great. We can—"

"Cut." This time it came from Marty. We both turned toward him. "Don't give specifics, just leave it as there will be a date tomorrow. I'll iron out the details and be in touch."

"Oh, sure," Dalton replied, a little flustered.

"Sorry," I whispered, sensing whatever moment we had was ruined. Marty would get an earful from me about that, but I always forgave him. The brand deals and sponsorships I'd gotten since putting him at the helm sweetened his bossiness.

We ran the scene back, then stood and hugged goodbye. I gave Patch some ear scratches and thanked him for being a gentleman while Dalton removed his mic. He shook Marty's and Harrison's hands on the way out in a way that was respectful and maddeningly wholesome, then left with his dog looking back over his shoulder like *call me.*

Once they were gone, my producer exhaled like a balloon you let go on purpose. "You were charming. He was charming. The dog was charming. We are up to our eyeballs in charm."

I wasted no time retrieving Winnie. "Say thank you to Uncle Harry for taking care of you."

She purred, and I failed to hide my surprise. "So, you like him now, do you?"

Harrison stayed quiet; he simply went about packing the gear, which was weird, because I'd said the Uncle Harry bit simply to get him riled, but he never took the bait. Contrastingly, Marty chatted through the entire breakdown about ratings and how he was going to be up all-night editing. He wanted to post the footage in the morning. On the short walk to the inn, he all but whistled with elation while throwing out date ideas.

When we arrived, Betty pressed foil-wrapped pumpkin bread and butternut squash soup into our hands and told us not to feed the third-floor ghost because it only encouraged him. We said good night to Marty, well I did. Harrison grunted.

SEVEN

Our suite was warm and upon entering, the radiator made a throat-clearing noise that read, in Mildred, as *well?*

I set the food on the mantel beside my smoky quartz. Winnie hopped from chair to chaise to floor conducting what I assumed was a thorough safety inspection while I poured her dinner into a bowl.

Harrison draped his jacket over the chaise and started setting up what he needed to dump audio.

Unable to take the quiet a moment longer, I blurted out, "What's your deal?"

"Excuse me?" He didn't look up.

"No, you're not excused. Why are you giving me the silent treatment?"

"I'm speaking with you right now. By definition that means I'm not giving you the silent—"

"Shut it."

He perched on the edge of the desk and crossed his arms. "Do you want me talking or do you want me quiet? Make up your mind."

The room divider was folded against the wall, so I

crossed freely over Switzerland territory and plopped onto his chaise. Why? Because I felt like it.

Harrison didn't protest.

"I think that went well," I declared, because we were having this conversation regardless of his willingness to participate.

"Good."

"Patch likes me."

"Low bar," he murmured, and then, because he is not entirely stone, he added, "but important."

"Anything you need to talk about? Observations? Comments? Concerns?" I asked, like we were coaching a team post-game.

He kicked one ankle over the other. "Marty's correct about ratings. Professionally, this has a high probability of being successful."

"Just professionally?" I thumbed over my fidget rings.

He didn't answer right away. The old pipes whistled. Winnie sneezed beside her bowl.

Finally, he yielded. "That is all I am equipped to comment on."

"Uh, no. We're friends now." I unzipped my boots and peeled them off.

Harrison hummed in agreement (I think) as he removed his glasses from the case and slid them on, clearly intent on proceeding with his work rather than having a conversation.

"Therefore, as my new bestie, you are obligated to talk through this prophecy stuff with me because I need to know if Dalton is my soulmate."

The tapping of his laptop keys stopped, and he actually glanced my way. "Soulmate?"

I made myself comfortable on his chaise and released an exasperated sigh. "The *prophecy*, Harry. Keep up."

He slid his glasses down the bridge of his nose. "There was no mention of a soulmate."

"I read between the lines."

"Soulmates are a construct of humanity. They don't exist."

I scoffed and slapped my hand against my chest as though he had fired a real shot. "You cannot be serious."

"Attraction is scientific. Chemical. Nothing more."

"Jeez, you're quite the romantic. How some woman hasn't scooped you up yet, I have no idea," I deadpanned.

"Attraction boils down to neurochemicals and hormones. Genetics can play a role in compatibility as well. I've told you, Siobhan, everything is science."

"Ever a skeptic," I muttered under my breath. Not having the bandwidth to argue further (because, hello, I had a ticking time clock on a *life changing* decision), I tossed up my hands. "Fine. Whatever. There is a lot riding on this for me, so call it what you will, all I need to know is what you think about Dalton and what you think he thinks about me."

He shrugged a shoulder. "I don't know him."

I clenched my jaw so hard my teeth hurt. That man would be the death of me eventually. "You were there. You heard our *entire* conversation. That means you know him as well as I do."

"Which is not a lot."

Winnie leapt onto the chaise and made herself comfortable on my lap. Petting her soft, tri-colored fur cooled down my Harrison-specific rage, which was like its own character living in my head. *Sit down*, I demanded. There was already enough running through my brain. I didn't need to deal with that little gremlin, too. Kitty purrs vibrated against my sacral chakra, and I closed my eyes, allowing it to soothe my nerves.

"Sorry." His voice was so low, I thought I'd imagined it. Either that or Mildred brought along a gentleman friend to haunt our suite.

My eyelids sprung open. "Did you say something?"

"If you need to talk about it, we can."

I should've known he wouldn't repeat that. It was a small miracle he'd even apologized to begin with. Actually, I couldn't recall another time I'd been on the receiving end of a *sorry* from him.

"You mean it? Because my mind is likely to enter a death spiral before midnight if I don't sort it all out."

He removed his glasses, folded in the arms, and placed them upside down on the desk. "This suite is a spiral-free zone."

A self-deprecating laugh expelled from my throat. "Have you met me? My business cards should read: *Shaunie Ross, Podcaster and Chronic Overthinker (not in that order)*."

His lips briefly curled up on one side, making it hard to distinguish whether it was a smile or a tic. "One thought at a time. What's the first one?"

"What did you think of him? And don't say you don't know him."

His fingers rapped on the desk. "He was nice."

"He was, right?"

"But I think he's after his fifteen minutes of fame." The words came out as though they'd been waiting behind his teeth for a while.

"What? Why?"

He shrugged. "Just my opinion."

That had me wondering if Dalton was only being nice because he wanted something from me. That wasn't totally off base given how awkward I'd been. I ran one hand from

Winnie's head to the tip of her tail, focusing on how her spine arched at my touch like a wave. "Do you think I was too...me?"

"You are a lot."

That hit directly on my core wound, and I recoiled. "Gee, thanks."

"Let me finish. You're a lot, but you're also...not a lot, if that makes sense." He grimaced. "It doesn't, does it? What I mean is you're not *too much*. You're *you*. If a man can't appreciate all of you, then he isn't yours. Simple as that."

The suite went still enough that I became aware of the pulse in my wrists. "Harry," I whispered, because it was either that or dump Winnie off my lap, rush across the room, and kiss him. And no, I haven't the faintest idea where that desire came from, so don't ask.

He cleared his throat. "Science. If you aren't on the same frequency as your partner, the attraction won't last."

"Careful. Frequency borders on woo-woo. You can't abandon your stoic skepticism now. It's your brand."

"Actually, frequency is science. As an audio engineer, my brand remains intact, thanks for your concern."

"Explain."

His brows arched. "You want to know?"

I shrugged, surprised by myself because I always tuned out whenever he talked about his work—it went over my head. "Sure. The distraction will reroute my brain from approaching the point of no return on the soulmate front."

He scooted the wooden chair back, rested his elbows on the arms, extended his legs under the desk, and crossed his ankles. "Everything you hear is a sound wave. You hear different tones and pitches when the sound waves vibrate at various speeds. The rate of movement is called frequency."

"So, what you're saying is that when I'm not vibing with

another person it's because our souls' frequencies are vibrating at different speeds?"

Harrison, being Harrison, dodged my direct question. "Higher frequencies correspond to higher pitches. Lower frequencies, to lower pitches. Opposing sound waves will cancel each other out." He gestured toward my nightstand where my e-reader, headphones, and tarot card deck sat. "Like those, for example. You wear them in a loud environment because they create silence, right?"

I nodded, trying to recall if I'd ever told him that. Too much noise would distract me, and I couldn't focus when I was overstimulated. Sometimes, being in large crowds completely paralyzed me.

"The noise-canceling technology works by creating an opposite sound wave to the incoming one, so you don't hear anything."

Winnie pawed my hand with an insistent meow to point out that I had stopped petting her and it was unacceptable. Her next swat would involve claws, so I gave a little scratch behind her ear. "You know, I think your science actually makes a little sense for once."

He gave me one of his signature eye rolls. "Science always makes sense."

The radiator let out a hiss like it was laughing at us.

"Mildred is that you?" I asked, mostly to further annoy my roomie.

"Do I need to explain the science behind hydronic heating systems, too?"

"Nope. We're still in the middle of our frequency lesson. You're telling me I need to find someone who has my same frequency, which basically means I'll be single forever." In my twenty-eight years, I'd never met someone who vibrated on my level.

"No, that's not true either."

"I'm confused."

He woke up his laptop and clicked the battery-operated mouse a few times. "Listen to this." A melody played through the speaker. "Now compare it to this." It was the same melody, but...richer. "Notice a difference?"

I nodded. "The second one has more oomph."

"Right." His face lit up the way one's does when discussing a passion. "I created a more complex sound by layering on a track that has double the frequency, meaning the second sound waves are moving at double the rate of the first ones."

"Wouldn't that make them opposing frequencies?"

"In a sense, yes, but there are other factors making them complementary."

"Like sound one and sound two have shared values, but different interests?"

This time, his smile was unmistakable. "Now you're getting it. We call this consonance. On their own, each sound is fine, pleasant, but together—"

"Like us," I blurted, because...filter. "We're opposing frequencies. Me and my chaos are up here." I held a hand above my head. "And you and your calm are down here." My other hand hovered above Winnie until she wrapped her paws around it, pulling me back for pets. "We balance each other. Synergy," I exclaimed.

He cocked his head. "Wait. Siobhan, are you saying—"

"That's why people love listening to our show. I'm a believer; you're a skeptic. I'm artsy; you're techie. I like pumpkin spice; you like boring coffee. But we have co...co..." I snapped my fingers in quick succession. "What'd you call it? Con-something?"

"Consonance."

"Consonance. Right." I grinned wide, proud of how I'd connected the dots.

He crossed his arms over his chest. "You pass the lesson. Dating, and I suppose podcasting, can be explained scientifically."

Dating...

I'd forgotten all about the point of his teaching moment. My cheeks warmed and I held in the groan that was clawing at the roof of my mouth because I'd accidentally insinuated that Harrison and I were compatible for a *romantic* relationship. We'd only been official friends for a day. Unable to look in my co-host's direction, I gave Winnie my full attention, which she thoroughly enjoyed.

I debated vacating the chaise and dragging the screen out, declaring Switzerland, because I needed a joke to deflate whatever balloon I'd accidentally inflated. Instead, I gathered the courage to glance his way and said, "Second date tomorrow." Because I was always the pin. "You don't have to come," I blurted, immediately hating myself for it.

Harrison's head flicked up so fast I felt the air move from across the room. "I'm coming," he declared, like I'd suggested something obscene. Then softer, "I mean, as long as you want me there."

I did. And didn't.

And did. "Yes, of course I do."

"Then I will be."

"Good."

The radiator ticked off the minutes like a nosy metronome. Eventually, Harrison donned his headphones, returning to work, and I stood, much to Winnie's dismay, and snagged my phone off the nightstand. I held the device in front of my face to unlock it as I sat on my bed (where I belonged).

There was a text message waiting.

Dalton: I had a great time tonight. Patch did too.

That should've made me smile, but the embarrassment from my conversation with Harrison must've been lingering, because nervousness filled me instead. I couldn't leave him on read—that wouldn't be nice—so I replied.

Me: It was fun. Patch is a sweetie.
Dalton: I knew I should've left him home. That dog always steals the show.

I wanted to ask him if this was all a show for him, even though he'd told me it wasn't at the end of our date, but Harrison's opinion echoed louder inside my skull. Before I could embarrass myself with a second man that evening, my phone chimed.

Dalton: I have a confession to make.

Another chime.

Dalton: I really wanted to kiss you.

Heat rose up my neck like someone had lit a match under my collarbone, and I suppressed the urge to sprint across the room, shove my phone in Harrison's face, and ask him what on earth I should say in response. "Pull yourself together," I whispered. I could flirt. I was *great* at flirting.

Reclining onto the pillows, I clicked to open my keyboard and typed, deleted, typed.

Me: I'll give you a pass. Kissing me in front of Patch probably would've been questionable Dog Dad etiquette.

Dalton: So you're saying I should leave Patch home tomorrow? Done.

Oh my God. Oh my God. Oh my God. My forearm fell onto my face, covering my eyes. Neurons fired haphazardly to my synapses, and I was barreling toward a full-fledged spiral.

Could tomorrow be the kiss Esme predicted?

Would my life be forever changed in less than twenty-four hours?

Forever is a long time.

What if I don't like the change?

My breathing bordered on hyperventilation.

Esme said the kiss would change everything, but she never said it would be a good change.

What if it's a bad change?

If I marry Dalton, I'll have to leave Boston and move to Sage Hollow and live on his orchard and—

"What's wrong?" Harrison's voice sounded far away, but that must've been on account of the blood pumping in my head making me disoriented because the mattress dipped beside me and someone pried my arm off my face.

The bright light stung, and I squeezed my lids shut as I shouted, "I don't want to quit the podcast."

"Why would you quit?"

"Because Dalton is going to kiss me tomorrow, fulfilling the prophecy, then I'll have to marry him and move here."

Harrison chuckled and it shocked me enough to crack open one eye (seeing is believing).

"I didn't know you could make that sound," I teased.

"I didn't know one kiss was the equivalent of a marriage proposal in the twenty-first century."

"Ever hear of Warren Jeffs?" I countered.

"Who?"

"Never mind." My problem took precedence over educating Harrison about religious cult leaders. I opened my other eye and scooted up to a seated position. "This is serious."

His face softened, which was easy to notice at such proximity. "The prophecy isn't real, Shaunie."

"Are you doubting Esme? Because last night you—"

"Permission to test my hypothesis?" He planted a hand beside my hip and leaned closer.

"Umm, okay, but your wron—"

His lips pressed to my lips.

And then they were gone.

I blinked a few times to determine if I was awake or dreaming. (Definitely awake.) "Did...did you just *kiss* me?"

He turned away and scratched at the ever-present stubble on his cheek. "Yeah."

I bounced onto my knees, which was not simple to do in a sweater dress, sending Winnie scurrying off the mattress with a hiss. "Why would you do that? The prophecy—"

"Isn't real. I just proved it. You don't think I'm your soulmate, right?"

My arms folded across my body. "Well, no."

"Exactly." He stood and went back to his desk where he unwrapped his pumpkin bread like nothing happened.

Once the shock dwindled, I went into the bathroom to shower and get ready for bed because the stress had stolen my appetite and left me exhausted. As I brushed my teeth, I opened the calendar on my phone and set a reminder to find Esme the next day, so I could see what Harrison's kiss meant for the prophecy.

Once in my Winnie-ween jammies, I moved toward the door but stopped short of opening it. Instead, I pressed my ear to the wood and heard Harrison's muffled voice. "Don't tell your mom I let you lick the spoon. And you should probably get down because if she comes out and sees you on my lap, she'll be jealous."

My hand cupped over my mouth as I pictured the cuteness in the other room.

Wait...

I didn't find Harrison cute. A chill tickled up my neck. *Could magic be at work already?* "Mildred," I whispered into the empty room. "What do you know about prophecies?"

The light above the sink flickered, but I didn't speak nineteenth century ghost.

I coughed, trying to sound natural, to announce that I was exiting the bathroom. In the main room, Winnie was on my bed, and Harrison was at the desk. He glanced up, his gaze dipping to my cat's giant witch hat-wearing face on my chest. I held up my hand. "Do not make fun. I love these."

A smile teased his mouth. "They're cute."

There was that word again.

"You should eat dinner," he said as I pulled back the comforter.

"Not hungry."

Once I was settled, Winnie pawed across my body until she found the spot she liked—on top of my shoulder in the crook of my neck.

Heavy footsteps crossed the room and the overhead light turned off.

"You can leave it on if you need."

"I don't."

The room was lit in a faint blue glow from his laptop screen and the wooden chair creaked under his weight.

I stared at the ceiling while somewhere in the wall, the pipes did their evening gossip. Downstairs, as if the inn itself liked to meddle, the foyer clock chimed nine times—a reminder that the day was coming to an end soon.

"Sleep well, Siobhan," Harrison said, soft, like a cozy blanket.

"You, too, Harry," I whispered back.

That night, the room divider stayed folded against the wall.

EIGHT

The morning after Harrison had kissed me to "disprove" the validity of prophecies, I pretended very hard that I had not been thinking about it. I failed. Repeatedly. Case in point, I stood by the window, clutching a paper cup of my leftover PSL and my dignity. *Leftover* PSL...Yeah.

I checked my phone for the hundredth time in thirty minutes. Ten o'clock on the dot, which meant the Ever After Emporium was open. "I'm going to see Esme," I announced with a little too much enthusiasm. (Desperation?)

"Okay." Harrison gave a small nod from where he sat working at the desk, seemingly unfazed by having derailed my destiny.

I stuffed Winnie into her carrier, shrugged on my vest, and made my way to the shop as quickly as I could without looking like a weirdo running down the street in Uggs while wearing a cat.

The bell over the door chimed politely. Esme looked up from behind the counter, braid over one shoulder, eyes warm enough to elicit confessions from strangers.

"Siobhan," she said, as though she'd been expecting me.

"I may have broken fate," I blurted. "With my face."

Her mouth curved. "Good morning."

"Right. Good morning." I hovered at the counter, then remembered how elbows worked and removed mine. "Your prophecy...I, um, ran a test. On accident. With Harrison."

Winnie bleated behind me in judgment.

"Oh?" Amusement danced in her expression—devoid of shock.

Stalling, I swung the bag off my back and placed my cat on the counter. "I kissed him. Well, actually, he kissed me."

"Good morning to you, Winifred." Esme stuck her crimson-painted, long, pointy nail through one of the holes on the side of the carrier and gave her a scratch, eliciting immediate purrs.

"Did you hear what I said?" I asked, trying to quell my panic. "*Harrison* kissed me."

"So, you said." She continued her cat scratches.

My thumb kept my fidget rings on a perpetual spin. "Harrison from my podcast." To keep from regurgitating my coffee, I placed a finger over my lips. *Traitors.*

"Did the sky fall?" Esme asked, calm as can be, as she retreated from Winnie.

"Not the sky. Just my brain. If your weathervane points north and I do donuts in the parking lot, can I still find north before the hurricane drowns me in the flood?"

"Prophecies point, yes. They do not push. And, last I checked, there are no hurricanes presently targeting New Hampshire."

"So, I didn't ruin the universe?"

"The universe is hard to ruin before noon." Her bracelets clicked softly as she struck a match and lit a candle beside the register.

"Is that noon today? Or noon in general. Because this was last night, so that detail matters."

Esme shook the match out, allowing smoke to breathe between us. "You're going to the festival tonight?"

"With Dalton. Yes." I'd woken up to a text from Marty with that proclamation. "How did you—? Never mind." In my line of work, I knew better than to be surprised by a psychic's *knowings*.

"Go. Let it be what it is." Her lack of alarm still had me on edge.

"But, Esme, I've already had my one kiss before All Hallow's Eve," I lamented.

"Something you must remember about prophecies is that each word has an intent." Her mouth formed a bemused smirk. "Yours foretold of one kiss, yes; however, there was no mention of you being limited to *only* one kiss."

A shell full of pewter angel wings caught my eye. It was right in front of me, yet I hadn't noticed it until just then. I plucked one up while I processed Esme's words and folded it into my palm. "That means there's a chance Harrison didn't block me from finding my soulmate, then, right?"

She stroked the quartz point hanging around her neck. "There's more to your prophecy that they are permitting me to share with you if you would like."

My eyes widened. "Yes, please."

She inhaled deeply, then blew it out with a sigh. "It tangles your life and his and what you *think* you're doing here. You'll have a choice."

"What sort of choice?"

"Between what you believe you *should* want..." She paused. "And what you actually do."

"Isn't the whole point of a prophecy for it to predict

what's meant to happen? Like, bloop, here's your soulmate." I dropped the wing on the counter to demonstrate.

"It's predicting that, following a kiss, you will have to make a choice. Free will is part of the beauty of a human experience."

"But I don't know what I want," I replied, although I'd intended to keep that bit to myself, but...filter.

"You will. Listen when the noise gets quiet."

"When the noise gets quiet," I echoed. If only she realized my brain was incapable of quiet. The bells chimed and I spun to see a group of college-aged girls enter. "Thank you for your time. I'll get out of your way." My arm looped through the strap of Winnie's carrier.

"Don't forget this." Esme held up the pewter wing.

"It's not..." My eyes dropped to the spot I'd gotten it from, but the dish was gone. "...mine."

"Yes, it is." She dangled the chunk of metal, insisting I take it, so I did.

Back on Middle Hollow Road, the cloudless sky gave the air that crisp, camera-ready quality that made even the trash cans look photogenic. I texted Marty that I was going to shoot some BTS for our socials and promised to hydrate like a responsible adult. He sent back three pumpkin emojis and an orange heart.

Wandering through the village, I contemplated what to do with the information Esme had given me. The footage from my first date with Dalton went live while I'd been in the shop, and my notifications had already maxed out. My followers would love to hear the rest of the prophecy, but something told me to keep it close to the vest. No pun intended, since I was indeed wearing a vest.

When I found a quieter section of the street, I opened one of my social media apps and went live. "Hey, guys!

Shaunie here. Welcome to Sage Hollow." I proceeded to give them a short tour and teased my festival date with Dalton, then repeated the process on the other four apps.

Come afternoon, I returned to the inn to find our suite empty. "Harry must've gone ahead to the festival with Marty to scout locations," I told Winnie as I unzipped her carrier. She stalked across the bed, making the little bell on her collar jingle.

It didn't take me nearly as long to prepare for the second date as I had for the first. Having finite outfit options made it easier than if I'd had my entire closet at my disposal. After freshening my makeup, I shrugged my fuzzy orange jacket over a pink, chunky knit sweater that matched the ends of my hair. "Come on, Winnie. Let's go."

She actively ignored me, choosing to remain curled up on Harrison's pillow.

"Winifred Sabrina Ross. I do not have time for this." I sighed as I zipped my knee-high black boots over my dark skinny jeans.

She didn't so much as twitch a whisker in response.

"I know you hear me."

The radiator hissed as I stomped toward the chaise. "If you won't listen to me, listen to Mildred."

Nothing.

Standing directly in front of her, I put my hands on my hips and tapped my toes on the carpet. Disappointing. It didn't make the same rewarding sound as it would have on wood. "Would you rather I leave you here with the ghosts?"

Her head perked up at that.

"I didn't think so." I turned and walked back to the bed followed by the quiet patter of cat paws.

. . .

THE FAIR HIT me like a cymbal crash.

Kids squealing in three different keys. Kettle corn, fryer oil, woodsmoke. Someone's perfume doing war crimes. My jacket was suddenly too warm, and my boots felt too tight, and the world was turned up to eleven with no volume knob in sight.

"I just have to make it to Marty and Harrison," I told Winnie, cinching her backpack to my front like armor.

I made it ten yards.

A fiddler hit a high note, a toddler let out a banshee shriek, and my brain did the Windows blue screen. I veered to a bench under a sugar maple and sat. Cold slats, sticky spot (caramel?), too-dry leaves crumbling under my boots. I pressed the heels of my hands under my headphones-that-I-stupidly-didn't-bring, which is to say, my ears. *Breathe in four, out six.* Count the orange mums. *One, two, three.* I lost count at the red flannel shirts.

Winnie butted the mesh with her head and gave me a low, offended meow that translated to *pull it together, human.* I slid a finger through one of the holes and she wrapped her paw around it, tiny claws grounding me better than meditation apps ever had.

"Hey." Harrison's voice came soft, low-pitched—studio tone, not street tone. He stepped into my peripheral, hands visible, not touching. "Can I sit?"

I nodded, and he took the far end of the bench like he knew the math of space. He didn't ask what was wrong. He just slipped a small case from his flannel pocket and popped it open revealing foam earplugs.

"New," he said, because of course he anticipated my germ brain.

I held out my palm. "Orange? It's giving festive. My ears do love a seasonal accessory." Humor came out automatic; gratitude landed a beat later. "Thanks." I rolled and tucked. The world dropped from a roar to a manageable hum.

"Better?" he asked. His eyes stayed on my face like he was watching audio levels.

I nodded. "I forgot my headphones." The admission felt like failure in my mouth.

"Crowd's denser near the entrance," he said, scanning. "Quieter if we cut behind the pumpkin wall, past the quilt booth. That'll get us to Marty."

"What are you doing here, anyway? Shouldn't you be with Marty?" I meant it curious, not accusatory, but it came out thin.

"I went looking for you. You weren't here when you said you would be." He gave a tiny lift of one shoulder. "Statistics favored overstimulation."

Some silly little knot in my chest loosened. "Nerd," I whispered, affectionate on accident.

He gestured toward my backpack. "Can I take the strap? Just to make a path."

"Yeah." I swallowed. "Please."

He hooked two fingers in the top strap of Winnie's carrier, not tugging, more like marking a tether. "Eyes on my shoulder," he said, and we stood.

He moved like a buffer, absorbing the shoulder bumps, calling quiet navigational notes. "On your left." "Step." "Curb." He angled his body between me and a stilt walker and quick-stepped us behind the pumpkin wall where the air calmed down. We had to step over a myriad of extension cords as we snuck between the back side of booths, but it was far more favorable than the alternative. We emerged to Marty. Harrison released my strap, and I checked that my hair was covering the earplugs.

"Hey, there you are," our producer shouted across the dirt walkway as he waved us over to a roped-off corner by the midway entrance. I was grateful for the false sense of security the plastic tape barrier provided.

Marty didn't miss a beat. "Quick rundown: B-roll while you two stroll, soft open, then I'll cue a short live segment. Fifteen minutes tops. You'll start here, circle past the cider stand, end at the hay-bale arch." He held up the body pack. "Arms?"

"Yep." I turned so he could thread the cord and clip the mic to my sweater.

Marty's hand slid toward Winnie's carrier. "I'll stash her—"

"She stays with Shaunie," Harrison said, even, no room for debate. He shifted an inch closer, easy wall against the crowd. "Her followers love the cat."

Marty squinted between us. "We don't want chaos on camera."

"Then don't create it," Harrison said, already tightening my transmitter clip like it was part of his job description. "Winnie's calmer with Shaunie. Our audio will be cleaner, not worse. Besides, the dog isn't coming."

I hugged the carrier.

Marty blew out a breath. "Fine. But you're flipping her to your back."

"Deal," I said.

Harrison adjusted my cable, and his gentle knuckles grazed the base of my neck, reminding me of how his lips had also been tender. *Gah!* The last thing I should've been doing was thinking about kissing him when I was about to go on a date with a different guy.

Harrison stepped back, eyes scanning the flow of people like he could shoulder-check the whole festival out of my way. "You're flushed," he said softly. "Relax. You're a pro."

I cleared my throat and straightened.

He hovered like he wasn't sure if he should leave me to my thoughts or hand them a helmet.

"Places in three," Marty called, already backing up with the camera. "Dalton's coming from the cider stand. We'll catch the approach."

A hayride rumbled past and I squared my shoulders, ready to smile like I hadn't melted down in the middle of the town's biggest attraction.

NINE

Dalton approached carrying two hot apple ciders like someone who thought he understood my particular brand of autumnal foreplay. PSLs they weren't, but apple sufficed.

His smile reached his eyes as he handed me one of the paper cups. "Hi."

"Hi," I managed.

"Ready to explore?"

"As long as you promise not to climb the outside of anything. Marty keeps threatening to go full Noah-and-Allie on me."

He laughed. It was easy; nothing performative about it. My shoulders dropped half an inch.

As we walked, my anxiety settled back into her hole. Not being alone in the crowd made it easier, as did the earplugs, albeit they made me miss a quarter of what Dalton was saying. I did a lot of nodding without knowing if I was agreeing to something egregious, like admitting dogs were better than cats. He asked about the podcast, Boston traffic, and Winnie (points for priorities). He didn't interrupt; a quality I appreciated because once someone derailed my train, I never got it back to the previous station. When I tripped over air—classic—he steadied my elbow and didn't make a joke at my expense.

Harrison listened to the whole conversation through his headphones while he floated at a respectful distance using my phone to collect BTS footage of string lights and strangers' laughter for me to edit into content later. His attention seemed to be everywhere but on me, and I didn't think I liked that very much.

"Ferris wheel?" Dalton asked. "Best view of the mountains."

"Only if you agree not to rock the bench. Sometimes Winnie gets motion sickness." I held my pinky up for him to promise, but he turned the other way leaving my littlest finger hanging in mid-air. *He must not have seen it.*

While in line, Marty clipped a GoPro contraption to my hand and gave me explicit instructions to pay attention to how I held it so not a moment would be missed.

"Not my first go with a camera, Dad," I jested while I moved Winnie's bag to my front.

"Do you want to leave her here?" Dalton asked.

"And deprive her of the mountain view?"

He laughed.

I wasn't joking.

We stepped onto the platform, and the ride operator caught the next bench, slowing it slightly, but it still hit the back of my knees with a jolt. The side of Dalton's jean-clad leg smushed up against my thigh, and I absorbed some of his heat, trying not to overthink about why I didn't feel a spark at the contact. Being that was the closest we'd physically gotten, I nervously fingered my hair to hide the earplug. I didn't need him seeing it and finding out I was weird.

You're not weird. My therapist's voice echoed in my head. *Fine, I'm quirky*, I corrected.

"What's that?" Dalton asked.

Gah! Did I say that aloud? "Umm, it was the cat." I patted the bag securely fastened to my torso. "We sound the same. Like mother like daughter." Embarrassed laughter bubbled from my throat.

At least he laughed, too.

My therapist didn't care much for quirky either. *What did Harrison say?* I recalled our conversation from the night before. Something about my ADHD not making my brain broken. *Operating system!* He'd called my ADHD my operating system. I liked that and was willing to bet my therapist would approve.

The seat swung of its own accord as we rose above Sage Hollow. From the top, the town looked like someone had shaken gold glitter over a postcard. I caught myself before I started talking to Winnie and pointing out the sights. Instead, I settled for squeezing her closer as the festival noise softened to a contented murmur. My brain, which usually played twelve tabs at once, clicked one or two of them closed.

"You're different in person than I thought you'd be," he said after a minute, almost apologetic.

"Uh, oh. Bracing for impact." I prepared for the incoming gut-punch.

"No impact. You can unbuckle your seatbelt."

"This high in the air? You monster," I jested.

He chuckled. "Different-surprising. I figured you played up this character for your videos and on your podcast, but it's real."

I wanted to ask a million questions about what that meant and if it was a good thing because it couldn't be, right? "Don't tell the internet," I whispered instead, resolving not to know. It would give me something different to overthink before bed. Inspiring a character in a book or movie would be cool, but *being* a character...

Ta-da. New rumination level unlocked.

The temperature fell rapidly as the sun inched behind a peak in the distance—a reminder of the darker winter days around the corner.

"You were right about the view," I noted.

"It's romantic." Dalton leaned closer, his face turned toward me, and I could *feel* what was coming next.

My heart hammered, which, thanks to my earplugs, sounded like a horror movie in my skull, and I began breathing like I'd sprinted a whole entire marathon. Was I ready for another prophecy kiss when I was still trying to sort out the first one?

Not even close.

Needing to break the moment, I looked away and cleared my throat. "How high up do you think we are?"

He hummed as he returned to his half of the too-small seat.

My manic pulse eased closer to neutral.

"Maybe seventy-five feet." He shifted, rocking the bench.

I gripped Winnie's bag a little tighter. "Harrison would hate this. One time, we were filming on location at this haunted tower in New Jersey; it was abandoned during construction because too many spooky things were happening so now it sits vacant and unfinished. Anyway, we were supposed to go up to the top, which was the thirteenth story—not a coincidence, BT-dubs—but the stairwell was open, like to the outside, you see, and Harrison refused to climb higher than the third floor. Even that was a struggle." I snorted at the memory. "He was funny, which isn't typical for him. Sometimes, I think he acts all moody simply to annoy me. I like it when he drops his mask, though."

Winnie meowed, sharp and punchy, one time. It was her way of getting my attention when I was in a brain spiral. *Was talking about Harrison spiraling?*

I cringed and inhaled sharply because, of course, rambling about him on a date was a major faux pas. Apparently, so was gasping on a Ferris wheel in forty-something degree temperatures because I choked on the air, spawning a coughing fit. I bent against the bubble window of Winnie's bag to try and cover it. She didn't love that so much, and protested by swatting the hard acrylic.

"Are you okay?" Dalton asked. He sounded concerned, which was sweet, especially considering my stupid word vomit about my friend. Who was a boy. Who wasn't him.

"Sorry," I managed, glad Harrison wasn't there to reprimand me. I would've had to argue that apology was warranted. So much so, that I said it again once I regained my composure. "Sorry."

"All good."

His reassurance felt hollow, and it left a trail of silence in its wake—the kind that came with cricket sound effects in movies. *Me and my stupid mouth.*

"Are you wearing earplugs?"

My muscles clenched. "They're a festive statement accessory. It's a new trend."

He hummed. "Must be a city thing."

Thankfully, there was a God (and She was on my side at the moment) because the ride slowed at the bottom, kicking us off. Back on solid ground, Marty rushed to meet us.

"Shaunie, did you hold your cat like that the entire time?"

I lifted a shoulder. "Maybe." It was the truest response because how could I remember a detail like that when I was too busy sabotaging my soulmate prophecy? Again!

He shook his head in disappointment. "The GoPro will be filled with up close monitoring of your calico. At least we have audio."

My eyes went wide. I'd forgotten *that* detail, too. I glanced around in search of Harrison, finding him over by a popcorn vendor, actively avoiding my gaze, headphones still firmly in place. He had heard Dalton's and my entire conversation...

Before I could process that, Marty ushered us toward the games. We wandered around doing festival things until the lamps blinked on and the whole place looked like it believed in magic. I terribly misjudged ring-toss physics, but Dalton redeemed us by winning me a tiny stuffed black cat (pity prize? charm offensive? unclear). He had big energy for a six-inch plush. I named him Salem before I could stop myself. We split a cider donut, which was more intimate than my inner germaphobe wanted to think about, so I didn't.

On the way past the buskers, a fire-breather exhaled too close and heat skimmed my arm. Harrison materialized behind me. "You good?" he asked, quiet. His palm flattened against the middle of my back—a brief barrier between me and the world—and my skin sizzled.

"I'm fine," I replied, my vocal cords like a tight violin string.

He nodded and vanished toward a lantern display, somehow both there and not. Dalton missed the moment because a kid squealed at a cotton candy cone the size of his head and we both laughed (for different reasons). Finally, we made our way toward our roped off area.

"I had a nice time. Thank you," I remarked out of politeness.

He gave me a goofy grin. "I did, too."

"Really?" My face scrunched up because I hadn't meant to say that aloud. Seriously, though, that date had been an awkward disaster.

"Really." He brushed a wisp of hair off my face, letting his hand linger.

My heart went into marathon-mode again as his head crept down.

He whispered, "Can I kiss you?"

I wracked my brain for an excuse. "It's No-Kiss October. Like Sober October but for mouths." *What is wrong with me?*

His brows dipped inward and his hand slipped from my cheek. "Huh?"

Marty appeared like an angel in tech gear, shedding his headphones. "Gotta love her sense of humor." He laughed a little too hard. "What Shaunie means to say is we need to build more tension for our audience. This isn't just a regular kiss—it's a prophecy kiss. Can't take that lightly."

I didn't love the mansplaining, but I suppose that one was warranted. Whatever got me out of another potential kiss with destiny. Marty earned himself a new novelty mug. *I wonder if Esme has any in her shop?*

Dalton smoothed out the front of his tan canvas coat. "I guess that makes sense."

"Great." Marty clasped his hands together. "I'd say that's a wrap. We can end on that little hair swipe maneuver. Leave things on a cliffhanger."

Moment smothered, we did the awkward dance of

goodbye where we hugged, but not too long. He shook Harrison's hand on his way past like a person raised by people who label Tupperware. Harrison's jaw ticked once. Neutral face, but opinionated eyes.

While I disentangled myself from my mic, Dalton had a quiet conversation with my producer behind the tape line.

"Do you think he's telling Marty he wants out?" I asked Harrison as I handed him my pack. "Because I wouldn't blame him, you know. Today was a disaster. I'm a disaster." It was easier to label myself broken than risk someone else deciding it for me.

Lifting one of the headphones' cups from around his neck, he put it to his ear and listened for a moment. "First off, you're not a disaster."

"Some people would disagree with you." My family had made an art form out of reminding me I was.

"People misunderstanding you does not make their opinion of you true. It makes them obtuse. Second," he continued like he hadn't just given my heart a hug with his words. "Dalton just asked Marty to tag his side business in the next video."

"What?" I ripped an earplug out, grabbed the other half of Harrison's headset, and smashed my cheek against his so I could listen too. Frowning, I said, "I don't hear anything."

Harrison swallowed and I felt it through my jaw because two people were not meant to be sharing the same headphones.

"Oh," I exclaimed as I jolted backward, releasing the earcup, smacking him in the side of the face with them.

"Jeez, Shaunie."

I covered my forehead with my hand. "Sorry. I didn't mean to. That or *that*." The apology spilled out before I could stop it—like it might buy me permission to stay.

"It's fine." He rubbed his cheek.

"Are you telling the truth?"

"Yes. It stings, but I'll survive."

I grunted. "Not your face, Harry. About you know who saying you know what." My chin lifted in their direction.

"Why would I lie?"

With my hands planted on my hips, I replied, "Maybe because you don't believe in this prophecy stuff, so you're trying to sabotage me just so you can be right."

He recoiled. "You think I would do that?"

"First, you kissed me," I whispered. "Which, I spoke to Esme about today. She said I can have more than one kiss, and the prophecy would still be true, so, ha! Joke's on you. And now this."

"Excuse me, miss." One of the vendors, an older gentleman with kind eyes and skin that suggested he'd spent too many of his years out in the sun, held up a white, leather cowboy (cowgirl?) hat with a pink feather tucked into the side. "This should be yours."

My frustration, the kind reserved specifically for Harrison, quelled at the unexpected interruption. "Excuse me?"

"My wife says it would look pretty with your hair." He gestured behind him to where his booth was set up.

"Oh. It's lovely." Despite not needing a hat like that, I tried it on anyway. The leather was butter-soft, and it settled into place like it knew my head—snug enough to stay on, loose enough not to give me a migraine.

"My wife was right." The man leaned closer. "But please don't tell her I said that."

I turned toward Harrison, but he'd gone behind the tape and was packing the equipment. "Do you have a mirror?" I asked the vendor.

"We sure do." He led me to his booth where I promptly

fell in love with a hat I didn't expect to love. After purchasing it, I returned to my crew. Thankfully, Dalton had left.

Marty gestured to my new accessory. "Not very you, but I like it."

"Thanks."

I waited for Harrison to acknowledge me. He didn't. It stung more than I wanted to admit.

"Good work today," Marty remarked.

I offered a weak smile in return. "What were you and Dalton talking about?"

"Logistics. Plans for the next date and such."

Next date? He hadn't even asked me. Did Sage Hollow operate on old school rules where plans were arranged through the woman's father? Because Marty wasn't my dad-dad. Just my work dad. Some people had work husbands; I had a work dad and... Harrison. Regardless, if I was going on a date, I wanted to be asked. I hummed. "That all?"

Marty picked up a gear bag and swung it over his shoulder. "Yeah. The guy is smitten with you."

I scratched my head, knocking my new hat off kilter. "How?"

"How what?"

Was I the only one on that date? Last I'd checked, there'd been an audience witnessing my train wreck behavior. Deciding to save that analysis for when I couldn't sleep later, I asked, "So, he didn't mention anything about social media?"

"Just that the orchard's page has gotten a lot of traffic from the video this morning. He asked me to tag his sled-making business in the next one."

My face flushed with heat, and I glanced at Harrison

out of the corner of my eye. He didn't so much as flinch. It was very un-Harrison to skip a told-you-so, which foretold it was going to be a long, tense golf cart ride back to the inn.

And it was.

TEN

The Honeymoon Suite had been turned down in our absence. Someone had straightened my hairbrush and tucked a coaster under my water without asking; the sort of small kindnesses that made me feel seen and, also, lightly judged. Life had taught me that even good intentions came with judgment. I set my new hat on the foot of the bed and Winnie hopped out of her carrier with a disgusted meow that said *finally*. I had a leash and harness, that she begrudgingly used, when necessary, but the festival had been too packed to risk her getting stepped on. She wasn't enamored with crowds either. Like her mom.

Harrison went straight to the desk and began unpacking his tech things.

Nope. My brain did not do unsaid things. "So," I said, toeing off my boots. "Are you mad at me, or are you auditioning to be in a museum exhibit called *Men Who Don't Have Feelings?*"

He didn't look up. "I've got audio to mix."

"That wasn't one of the options."

A slow exhale. He set his laptop down. "I'm not mad."

"Okay," I said, because I am mature, then I continued, "You didn't look at me for the last, like, hour."

"I was trying to get us out of there quickly."

"You also didn't gloat about being right re: the social media thing, and petty victory laps are your comfort hobby."

That got me the tiniest flick of a glance. "I didn't 'gloat' because it wasn't appropriate."

"Appropriate," I echoed, while dumping a scoop of food into Winnie's bowl. She rewarded me by rubbing up against my legs. "Cool, cool, cool."

When he didn't offer more, I tried a different approach. "Hey, thanks for running interference. And for not being weird about it."

"I was weird," he said.

"Familiar weird."

Nothing.

"I'm sorry, but if you're not mad, what are you?"

"Tired." He dropped onto the desk chair, emphasizing that point.

I did my best game show buzzer impersonation. "Try again."

He rubbed the bridge of his nose. "Conflicted," he said finally, his mouth forming a small, reluctant line. "Watching you almost kiss a guy on a Ferris wheel while I monitored the noise floor was not my favorite task."

My heart did a slow, traitorous roll. "Are you saying you were jealous?"

"That's not a precise metric."

"It's a feeling, Harry, not a statistic. Feelings don't need peer review to be considered valid."

He huffed a sound that wasn't quite a laugh.

I sank onto the edge of the bed and Winnie immediately commandeered my lap like she owned the mortgage. "For the record, I didn't want to kiss him."

"We helped you get over the prophecy pressure last night, no?"

The mere mention of his kiss set off my belly bats. "That wasn't why."

"What then?"

I'd been wondering the same thing all night. "Findings inconclusive."

"You can use science for feelings, but I can't?"

I reclined onto one hand (the other was occupied with petting Winnie—obvi). "I just didn't *want* to."

His gaze finally found my face and stayed there, making my spine tingle. "Then you don't do it. You set the pace, Siobhan. On or off camera."

The words landed soft and heavy, like a blanket I hadn't realized I wanted. "Thank you."

Knock. Knock. Knock. The sound came from behind my bed, three sharp taps in a triangle pattern.

"Hi, Mildred," I acknowledged. Even Winnie was getting used to the suite's quirks; she barely stirred.

"Plumbing," Harrison murmured, but his voice lacked conviction.

"About the prophecy," some unknown force nudged me to say. "Esme told me this morning that there's more to it."

His brows arched, which was an interesting reaction for someone who thought it was a bunch of baloney. "Did she say what?"

"That why I believe I'm here and why I am here are different things. I'll have to make a choice between what I think I should want and what I actually do."

He scratched at the stubble on his jaw. "What does that mean?"

"Don't know yet. But I'm not sure if I'm supposed to," I added, recalling how she'd mentioned I'd understand if I listened when the noise got quiet.

Harrison rapped his knuckles on the desk. "Isn't a prophecy meant to be definitive?"

"That's what I said," I exclaimed, a little too enthusiastically, I guess, because Winnie made her displeasure known with a curl of her claws into my leg. "Ouch, Winifred Sabrina Ross. Rude."

She yawned.

Harrison shook his head. "You're admitting it's bogus, then?"

I held up a finger. "No. Esme said the prophecy is that I will need to make a choice because I have free will."

"Siobhan, you realize, by nature, that's every relationship."

"Not *every* one." I pouted. "A woman could be held hostage and end up in a relationship with her captor. That's more force than choice."

He rolled his eyes. "Don't tell me you read dark romance books."

"What? No, that's the plot of *Beauty and the Beast*."

He hummed. "At the end, doesn't he let her go and she *chooses* to come back?"

"Wait a sec—" I leaned forward. "Do *you* read dark romance?"

"I have a sister."

"You do?" That hadn't come up in my internet deep dive on him.

"No." He opened his laptop and stared at it. "Only child."

Holy plot twist! "Oh my God, you totally read them! And—hold up—did you just tell a joke *and* share something personal?" I fanned myself. "This is a lot from you in one go. I'm not sure I can handle it."

"Don't hurt yourself. I saw some posts about it on socials."

"Not sure if I believe that, but I'll take it because you're sharing, *friend*."

He cleared his throat. "Umm." Then he stopped, which is how you knew it mattered.

"Yes, Harry?"

"On the Ferris wheel, you said you like it when I 'drop the mask.'"

Heat crawled up my neck. "You heard that, huh?" It was a stupid question with a blatantly obvious answer, but it was the best I could do.

"Headphones," he said, a little wry. Softer, he added, "I don't mean to wear a mask."

"It's okay if sometimes you do. It's heavy being a person. Armor happens."

Winnie kneaded my thigh like a tiny pastry chef, and something poked me (not her claws). I stuck my hand in my pocket and retrieved the offending object: the pewter angel wing. I didn't recall putting it in there. *Weird.*

"Yeah," Harrison replied on an exhale, reminding me that we were mid-conversation.

I closed my hand around the wing. "But you're allowed to feel things with me, you know? You don't have to label them like your audio files first."

He looked at me for a long second, the way he looks at a waveform he's trying to decide whether to cut or keep. Something in his expression unlatched—not a floodgate, just a latch.

"I wasn't always this way," he said. Not defensive. Simply true.

A hundred questions clamored for the front of my mouth: *What happened? When? Who hurt you?* But I swallowed them all, because somewhere low in my chest, I already knew the answer—maybe not the details, but the shape of it. Grief. Disappointment. Something sharp enough to make him armor up for good. My brain wanted to make a joke, throw him a lifeline shaped like sarcasm, but my gut told me to sit still and let the quiet do its work. "Since when?"

His gaze slid to the dark windowpane that held the town in a soft reflection. "Another time."

"Okay," I said, because pushing would make the latch snap shut. "Another time."

He stood, slipped his hands into his pockets like he didn't trust them unsupervised. "I'm going to take a walk."

"It's cold. Bring a scarf." It was my way of saying *be careful* without being annoying.

He picked up the one draped over the chair back. "I might grab food. Want anything?"

"Surprise me."

"Okay."

"Just not popcorn. Or candy apples. Or apple cider donuts."

He snorted. "Sure."

"And nothing fried."

He shrugged on his coat. "Got it."

"Also—"

"You want sushi, Siobhan." Not a question, but a statement.

My stomach gurgled its approval. "That's perfect. But the rolls—"

"Have to have the same number of pieces and be in separate containers. I know."

That was one of my weird quirks. I would eat one piece from each tray, in order, that way there was always the same amount of each type. I hadn't realized Harrison had noticed that about me before. It made my cheeks tingle with warmth. "Thanks."

At the door, he hesitated. "For the record, I don't act moody to annoy you."

"Oh, so the annoyance is just a bonus? Lucky me."

His shoulder did a tiny shake as he exited, leaving me with Salem and a calendar that suddenly felt very close to Halloween.

ELEVEN

The day had been all autumn spices, wool scarves, and pretending I knew the difference between Ceylon and cassia in a blind taste test. Spoiler: I did. Not because I was a savant but because I'd inhaled enough cinnamon that week to qualify as a blood type. Cinnamon Positive. Harrison had rolled his eyes when I'd announced that discovery, which meant I'd won, obviously.

That afternoon, Harrison and I had been guest judges for the pumpkin pie contest. It was a tough job, but someone had to do it, right? I may or may not have also taken some back to the suite with me for later because paranormal investigating always made me work up an appetite. A little sweet and spooky.

Come evening, I was more than ready to explore the section of the inn that, by all accounts, sane people avoided. People thought I chased ghosts for thrills. Really, I chased them because I understood the need to be noticed, to be acknowledged. Sometimes, even after death, you just wanted someone to say, 'I see you.'

"Remind me again why we're doing this?" I asked as we

stood in the lobby of the inn, watching our private tour guide—a college-aged woman in a velvet cape and combat boots—set up a portable lantern like she was about to lead us into battle. It was giving *Wednesday Addams: Outdoor Adventure Edition.*

"Because you love it," Harrison replied, tugging the zipper of his jacket higher. His tone was clipped, efficient, like we were about to file taxes instead of go ghost hunting. "As do our listeners."

"And because you're dying to debunk," I added, poking his arm. "Don't act like I don't know you packed half of GhostStop in your bag, roomie."

He didn't deny it. Which was as close to a confession as I'd ever get from him. Old habits died harder than vampires at sunrise.

"Shaunie, give us an intro," Marty nudged me closer to the door that had a sign posted on it reading, *No Entry Beyond This Point (Management Not Responsible for What Follows).*

Pulling my braided pigtails to the front of my shoulders, I cleared my throat and waited for Marty's cue. "Welcome back, spooky friends. Tonight, Harrison and I are ignoring common sense, OSHA recommendations, and this very official-looking *Do Not Enter* sign to bring you inside the haunted wing of the Sage Hollow Inn where guests supposedly check in, but not out. Yes, my co-host is already rolling his eyes. If we vanish, please tell Winnie I love her."

"Golden." Marty grinned. Deep down, he was a ghost junkie, too.

I spun my rings. "Should I have made a contingency plan for Winnie in case something really does happen to me tonight?" Much to my chagrin, I'd left her in our suite since she'd been cooped up in the bag on my back all day.

Harrison had said something about it being cruel to deprive her of stretching her legs and cuddling on my pillow, so in the room she stayed. Sometimes, the guy was right. Not often, but sometimes.

He shook his head. "You'll be fine, Siobhan."

"Maybe I should go get her. She might be scared in our room with all the noises."

"She'll be fine, too."

"You don't *know* that."

He pulled his cell out of his pocket. "Would you feel better if Betty stops in to check on her?"

I nodded vigorously.

He made the call and arranged it. When they hung up, he said, "Betty is going to bring her homemade cat treats."

That eased my anxiety some, but not much.

Harrison took a step closer, his voice calm like a captain leading his crew through a storm. "I'll be your ESP tonight, okay?"

My head tilted. "Extrasensory perception? A few days in Sage Hollow and you go from being a skeptic to a psychic, huh?"

"No," he deadpanned. "Emotional Support Person."

My chest zipped tight, and for the first time, I noticed a warmth in Harrison's typically guarded eyes. He meant it. If I stared too long, I might start believing he could actually see me, which was scarier than any poltergeists residing in the inn.

Before I could begin to process that, our guide, Raven Blackwood (not her real name, I'm guessing), raised her lantern. Her voice dropped into that hushed, campfire storyteller register. "This wing hasn't housed a guest in over a century. Some say it's because of faulty wiring. Others say..." She paused dramatically enough to earn an Oscar. "The residents never left."

Marty, crouched behind his camera like a caffeinated gremlin, gave her a thumbs up. "That's money. Keep it rolling."

I popped open my small case and ran a quick sweep. EMF: baseline low. Temp gun: steady sixty-seven. "Quick baseline," I told my recorder, narrating automatically. "If we catch anything later, I want a clean comparison."

Raven led us to the closed-off hallway. "There's no electricity in this area."

"Prudent," Harrison noted as he kept step beside me. "Why add to the bill if this area stays vacant."

"Oh, that's not it," Raven corrected. "The spirits here prefer darkness, so they keep it this way." Shadows lapped against the edges of the hall like ink in water. "This wing was once the pride of the inn. It was added on as a private residence during the Gilded Age after a wealthy mill owner named Thaddeus Pryor purchased the building. He was known for excess: lavish parties, imported wines, diamonds for his wife simply because it was Wednesday."

She paused at a framed portrait of a stern-faced man with a jaw that could've been used as a construction tool. "But the Pryors' youngest daughter, Eleanor, grew ill with fevers. Doctors couldn't cure her. Some say Thaddeus made a bargain—more wealth for her health. It's believed he locked her in her room when her mind began to wander."

My heart broke for her at that. No one deserved to be locked away—a prisoner of their thoughts. I shivered.

The lantern's glow danced across peeling wallpaper.

"They found her at sixteen. She'd starved." Raven let the silence breathe just long enough before adding, "Her room was this way."

My EMF ticked up. A polite blip. My skin prickled.

"Of course," Raven said with a sly smile, "sometimes guests report seeing her around the property. A thin girl in white, hair uncombed, eyes hungry. Since she spent her life alone, she has been known to lock people in here, forcing them to keep her company."

Behind me, Marty whispered gleefully into his mic, "Spooky."

This was the kind of story that was catnip for our listeners: dark history, tragedy, possible residual haunting. "Residual versus intelligent is the question," I muttered to my recorder. "If you can hear me, Eleanor, three knocks?"

Silence.

Then a door down the hall slammed.

I nearly jumped out of my sheepskin boots. *Residuals first, panic later.* "Okay," I breathed. "Tagging that."

"That's her room. Where she was found by the chambermaid," Raven explained as we made our way to the offending door.

My brows shot up. "Chambermaid? I don't suppose you know what her name was, do you?"

Harrison rolled his eyes and groaned.

Raven hummed, seeming to search her memory. "I'm not sure, but it might be in the souvenir book in the gift shop next door. It's called, *Sage Hollow Inn: A Haunting History.*"

"I bet her name was Mildred," I gleefully announced, elbowing Harrison, before speaking into my tape recorder, "Reminder: Buy souvenir book."

At Eleanor's door, I checked the air flow, hinge slack, and floor pitch.

"Draft," Harrison muttered, crouching to check.

"Plausible," I agreed, sweeping the jamb with the temp

gun. "Logging the timecode anyway. If it repeats, that's interesting."

"From what? The Phantom HVAC?"

We moved into what Raven called the parlor room. A chandelier dangled above, half its crystals missing. Beneath it hung sepia-toned photographs of the Pryors, all grim, as though the photographer had charged more for smiling.

And then the EMF shrieked.

"Phones to airplane mode," I ordered. Mine was already set. Harrison obeyed for once. *Growth.* I scanned outlets and sconces. The spike stayed. One of the family photographs on the wall tilted. Just a fraction. But enough.

"Okay." My voice wobbled as I pressed a hand to the baseboard to test for vibration. "Could be warped wood," I whispered, not wholly believing it.

Even Marty stopped narrating, his lens fixed on the photo like he expected Eleanor herself to step through. His camera whirred. "Please tell me you saw that."

"I did." My pulse stuttered, and my recorder light blinked red. On playback, there was faint humming. *A lullaby.* The tune was so soft it might have been mistaken for static if not for the cadence.

I froze. It was almost familiar. The rise and fall of the melody tugged at something buried in my memory, but the harder I reached for it, the further it slipped.

"That's a child's song," I whispered. Cold swept down my arms, though I couldn't say if it was the recording or the strange pull of déjà vu. Like I should've known it. Like I'd heard it before.

Fascination overrode fear even as cold swept down my arm. "That's a child's song." Another photograph crashed to the ground with a heavy thud. Someone screamed (me?) and I jumped into the steady chest of my ESP. Harrison grabbed my recorder. His fingers lingered around mine before retreating too carefully. "You okay?" he asked, not a hint of sarcasm present.

I took a few steps away from him, returning to safety. "Yeah. Can I have the thermal imaging camera?"

He handed it over.

My breath caught.

The EMF beeped again.

Something rustled down the hallway.

"Anyone hear that?" I asked, closing my eyes to heighten my hearing. Creaking. Like bare feet on old wood. My eyelids popped open, half-expecting to see Eleanor standing there, but no.

Marty was nodding, nostrils flared, shaking the camera with his movement.

"Residual," Harrison said automatically, but there was an unevenness in his tone that suggested even he wasn't convinced.

"Or intelligent." My throat felt dry. "Eleanor? If that's you, we see you."

The chandelier above us trembled, one crystal clinked distinctively, like an answer.

I swallowed. "Thanks for letting us walk through," I said softly into the cold room. "We'll tell your story respectfully."

I logged the crystal tremor, though my data was already conclusive. The real anomaly was the way Harrison steadied me without hardly trying. Paranormal spikes I could explain away. Him? Not so much.

WE MADE it back to the Honeymoon Suite alive, which felt like an accomplishment worth celebrating with mulled wine and a good sage smudging. Winnie's tail flicked in disdain from her perch on Harrison's pillow. Not mine. His. I crossed the room and scooped her up. "See, she's mad at me for leaving her. I told you."

Harrison set his gear on the desk. His mouth twitched like he was fighting a smile. "Is she mad at you? Or are you mad at me for convincing you to leave her?"

I scratched between her ears. "Both."

"Was I insufficient in my duties as your ESP?"

"I mean, when the photo tried to murder me, you were ready to sacrifice me to save the equipment."

"Is that how you interpreted it?"

"I launched myself at you, seeking *emotional support*, and you responded by taking the recorder away from me, so..." I trailed off, letting the absence of conclusion speak for itself.

He pulled the device out of his bag and held it up. "I took it so you could focus on yourself instead of your precious readings." His eyes lifted to mine, steady and dark. "It's replaceable. You're not."

Gulp. The bats in my gut were rumbled awake like they'd been sleeping beneath an angry volcano. I urged my brain to come up with something funny to say, but the traitor was stunned into silence for once. I didn't know what was more shocking: the lack of static in my skull or Harrison's statement. Winnie yawned like she couldn't care less that my entire emotional landscape had just been remodeled.

Harrison put the recorder on the desk with a thud.

Ten seconds ticked by—I counted them by my heartbeats. Then twenty. Have you any idea how long twenty seconds of silence is in a room zinging with tension? A hundred hours is the correct answer. *Lub-dub. Lub-dub.*

Half a minute of total silence. It was too late for a response then, even if I could come up with one.

My emotional barometer in feline form finally sensed my awkwardness because she squirmed in my arms and insisted on being put down, so I carried her to the bed. "Well," I croaked, sinking onto the mattress. "That was horrifying. Ten out of ten, would recommend."

He hummed with an undercurrent of something. Disappointment?

Sorry formed on the tip of my tongue, but I bit it back as I kicked off my boots. "That was exciting, right?"

"Sure." He removed the memory card from one of the cameras and inserted it into his laptop.

I took a bite out of the air, letting it puff out my cheeks while I breathed through my nose. Why? Because I was weird. Quirky. No, because I was running a different operating system.

So, if I wanted to cope by impersonating a chipmunk, then that's what I would do.

And then Harrison crossed the room. Direct. Unflinching.

My cheeks deflated like a popped balloon.

"What's exciting is science," he said as he came to stop a hair's width from my knees.

"How can you still be skeptical after an experience like that?" Before thinking things through, I stood, putting his clavicle in my line of sight.

"That's not what I am referring to." He was close enough for me to feel his breath on the top of my head. It smelled like cinnamon gum; my favorite.

"Oh. What science excites you then?"

"Chemistry." His voice dipped to an octave I felt in my bones, and his pupils flared.

It hit me then—all at once—like a microburst, appearing without warning and with a ferocity capable of downing every chaotic tree planted in my head. *Attraction is chemical*, his words from the other night echoed inside my decimated skull.

I was *attracted* to Harrison. My co-host/friend/roomie, Harrison. Mr. Skeptical-on-a-good-day, arrogant-on-a-bad-day, Harrison.

"Don't spiral, Siobhan," he whispered as the back of his finger traced a line down my cheek, leaving 4th of July fireworks over the Charles River-sized sparks in its wake. "Or, if you do, take me with you."

With reckless abandon, I threw my arms around his neck, dragging him into my chaos. My lips found his, or his found mine, I don't know. But this time, I was prepared for it. Wanting it. Craving it. Craving him.

This time, he was not tentative. Not testing. Just, full. Consuming. Like he'd been restraining for weeks and finally let it out. This wasn't a kiss for the sake of a soulmate prophecy science experiment.

My fingers slid into his hair, tugging him closer, and his hand cupped my jaw, thumb rubbing gently. The world tilted. No—I tilted, falling backward onto the bed, dragging him with me. His shirt rode up, warm skin under my palm. My sweater slipped off one shoulder. The air burned around us with agonizing need.

His mouth skated over my jaw and down my neck, pressing the detonator to my brain. This activity did not require thinking, only feeling. So, I let myself feel. The ticking of seconds gave way to counting his kisses as he warmed a trail from my ear to shoulder. My skin reacted by sending electrified neurotransmitters to my neurons. It was what Pop Rocks candy felt like, but everywhere.

He rolled just long enough to nudge my sweater up to my chin before introducing his lips to my décolletage. His stubble scraped against my thin skin, providing a stark contrast to the gentle warmth of his lips. Harrison slid a hand behind my back and, after a couple attempts, unhooked my bra, which I promptly discarded.

"What the—?" He pushed up over my torso and gazed down at my bare breasts. "Are these rocks?" He scooped up the collection stored in my cleavage.

"Crystals." I cupped the side of his head and stroked his earlobes.

"You keep them in your boobs?" Amusement danced across his eyes.

"Sure do." My fingers threaded into his hair. "If you're done judging, could we get back to the kissing part?"

He smirked and touched his lips to my forehead. "Whatever you want."

I licked his Adam's apple. Why? Because I felt like it. He didn't complain. His lips met mine again, and he parted them with his tongue while his hand cupped my breast. I moaned into his mouth.

This is happening. This is—

BANG.

The radiator in the corner shuddered violently, metal clanging like a poltergeist drumline had picked that precise second to rehearse. Winnie bolted under the bed.

"We should log that," I gasped, even as my pulse galloped. "Hydronic knock is common, but—"

Harrison's look silenced me. Hunger and... something else. Something darker.

We both turned to stare at the radiator like it had personally ruined our lives.

"Well," I said after approximately three eternities. "That was..."

"Yeah." His voice was gravel. His forehead rested against mine for a beat, as though he was as incapable of moving as I felt.

Finally, he eased back. His gaze softened. "It's not the right time."

Was the darkness I'd seen in his eyes regret?

My heart panged.

"No," he whispered into my hairline, as though he'd read my mind. "Timing, pumpkin. Only timing." The way he said it, like he wasn't feeling doubt at all, made me wonder, regardless of the when, if it could ever really be wrong.

Also... *did he just call me pumpkin?*

Cue the bats.

TWELVE

The orchard was a living, breathing Pinterest board. Rows of pumpkins glowed like they knew they were the stars of the show, strings of triangle bunting flapped, and a donkey heehawed in the petting zoo. Marty jogged backward in front of us, camera in hand. "Okay, okay. Today is a vibes day. Laugh. Touch a gourd. Don't antagonize the local PTA. We go live in thirty."

"I'm very pro-PTA," I said, adjusting the position of my mic. "Love a bake sale."

Marty gestured toward the corn maze. "I'm going to grab a few shots before we begin."

Once we were alone, Harrison said, "We need to decide boundaries for Dalton on-camera."

It had already been a tense morning, and we hadn't gotten to the hard part yet. Or any part, truly. I'd barely had any of my morning PSL, delivered to me in bed by Harrison (swoon!), when Marty had called and dropped a bomb. Not only had he given me fifty-eight measly minutes to get ready for a date I'd never been asked on, but he'd decided the entire thing would be live streamed on our socials. Something about engagement and followers and ratings.

The content creator in me recognized his genius, but my inner hopeless romantic with a soulmate prophecy and a co-host situationship looming over her was on the verge of panic. I would've been in full-blown panic mode had I been given enough time to think beyond my hair (messy bun, but chic), makeup (natural warmth), and fashion (mustard-colored sweater, black leggings, tan Ugg boots, and Winnie on my back), but no—

"Shaunie," Harrison quipped. "Focus."

"Sorry." As I turned to face him, I tripped over my other foot but caught myself. "What were you saying?"

"Boundaries."

"Boundaries?"

"With Dalton."

"Dalton?"

He rolled his eyes. "Are you going to keep repeating everything I say?"

I got my rings spinning at a decent rate. "Sorry."

"You and that word."

"Fine, I'm not sorry. Boundaries with Dalton. Go."

"He's part of the story," Harrison said, too casual.

"Great. Love that for us." I pasted on a smile that probably looked like I was smelling a suspicious cheese. "What do you suggest I do if a man lunges at my face with romance?"

"Deflect," he said, clipped. "Kindly. For your brand."

"Like you deflected last night?" It slipped out before I could file it for later.

His jaw ticked. "We're working."

"Right. Work." I was too under-caffeinated and too overstimulated for this conversation to go well.

Boisterous kids ran in cider-scented loops behind him screaming about bouncy houses, while their parents negotiated treaties with donuts. I was not envious of the parents or the kids.

"Do you want children?" I asked, as though it wasn't completely inappropriate.

"What?"

"Kids, Harry." I mimed rocking a baby. "Do you want to make them?"

His jaw ticked and the slightest hint of pink poked through his stubble.

"Oh, God." I slapped my palm to my forehead. "I didn't mean—not like, *make* them right now. Unless you're wanting to practice, in which case, I think I could maybe be available perhaps."

"Could you 'maybe be available perhaps' for this *work* conversation?" It was a grumpy Harry kind of day. He probably hadn't had enough coffee that morning either.

I held up a hand in surrender. "Present and available."

We were adults. Professionals. Two adult professionals who had nearly rearranged each other's molecules against a haunted headboard the night before. Not a big deal. We could discuss work instead. Totally.

Dalton spotted us from behind a mountain of decorative corn and lifted a hand, grin already in place. The man looked like Jennifer Lopez herself had wished him into existence for a cheesy 2000s rom-com, with his flannel, forearms, and clean shave. Patch the golden retriever bounded at his side, tongue out, ears flying like joy flags.

"Hey." Dalton pulled me into a one-armed hug that smelled like woodsy soap and hay.

Patch wagged his tail like he could power a wind farm,

so I rolled up my too-long sleeve, knelt, and offered my hand. "Hi, cutie."

He took that as a written invitation to moisturize my entire forearm. One warm, enthusiastic swipe from wrist to elbow. "Okay. Boundaries are a suggestion, I see." I wiped a glossy strand of drool on my black leggings and immediately regretted it.

Winnie meowed in a tone that demanded acknowledgment from her throne on my back.

"Friend," I told her, swinging the bag to my front so she could inspect the situation personally. Patch zeroed in, nose first. He fogged the acrylic window with two cheerful huffs, then booped it like a doorbell.

Winnie hissed so hard the entire bag bowed. She executed a rapid-fire series of karate taps that said, *absolutely not,* in sixteen languages.

"Patch, gentle," Dalton warned, already shortening the leash. Patch obeyed for exactly half a second, then play-bowed, front paws splayed, back end pogoing like a jack-in-the-box that had found religion. His helicopter tail clipped my thigh, smacked my mic pack, and produced a static squeal in Harrison's ear. He was less than thrilled.

Marty laughed with delight as he framed the chaos like it was cinema.

"Hold on," I muttered, trying to keep the backpack steady. Winnie rose to her full nine-pound height, arched into a Halloween decoration, and fluffed to the size of a throw pillow. Patch, thrilled by this theatrical performance, attempted a very polite nibble of the zipper pull. I pivoted to block. The strap slid off my shoulder. Somewhere in the shuffle, Patch's leash looped my ankle.

"Cats and dogs. Statistically, not ideal," Harrison said, already stepping in. His hand landed at my waist to steady me as I did a one-legged flamingo to keep from eating hay. With his other hand, he nudged the bag upright and away from Patch's very boopable face. "I've got her," he declared, with an authority that had me pausing to swoon.

Winnie, seemingly taken by him as well, stopped mid-hiss to glare through her bubble window, then went quiet, like, *fine, you may assist my staff.*

"Patch, sit," Dalton said, voice firm. Patch sat. His whole back half continued wagging independently, as if the word sit did not legally apply to hindquarters.

"See?" I told Winnie, breathless, as I freed my ankle. "He's a gentleman."

She tucked her paws, settling like a queen who had acknowledged a peasant and would not be doing so again. Patch answered by sneezing on my leggings. Or rather *his* leggings, because between his golden fur and bodily fluids it was safe to say he was their new owner.

"Two minutes to live," Marty announced.

"Does anyone have a lint roller?" I pleaded with everybody in a twenty-foot radius while I did my best to knock off Patch's love-dusting.

A mom came to my rescue, and I accepted her lint roller like a sacred relic, swiping until the static could've powered the Ferris wheel.

Harrison, still holding Winnie, remarked, "Cute show." His eyes lingered on me, but I didn't have time to soak it in.

I did a little twirl. "Am I good?"

Harrison flicked a glance over my outfit like a TSA agent. "Almost. Behind your left knee."

I swiped. "Now?"

"Other left knee."

I swiped again. Patch attempted to intercept the used roller sheet like it was a flying snack. Dalton reeled him back with a cheerful, "Leave it, buddy." Patch obeyed for half a second, then sneezed fur into the wind like a glitter cannon.

Winnie sneezed, clearly filing a complaint with management.

"I quit." I handed the roller back to the mom in defeat.

"Mics are good to go," Harrison noted. "Try not to wrestle any more mammals."

"No promises." I huffed. "Actually, would you mind watching her? I don't have it in me to repeat that."

"Already planning on it." He swung the strap over his shoulder.

"Thanks." I fussed with my hair. "How's my dignity?"

"Borderline," he deadpanned.

Marty clapped. "Positions! Shaunie will open by the entrance to the corn maze, do the big reveal, then move through the pumpkin patch. Keep it bouncy. Keep it PG. PG-13 tops. I am begging you."

"Define PG-13," I requested, but the countdown was already ticking.

Marty held up his fingers. *Three. Two. One.*

"Hey, spooky friends! We're coming to you live from the Wakefield Family Pumpkin Patch and Orchard, where the cider is hot, the donuts are sweet, and the pumpkins are trying their best to look like they belong on your porch. I'm Shaunie, and with me is the orchard's MVP, Dalton, and employee of the month, Patch."

"He works for treats."

"Same." I began our 'leisurely stroll,' as Marty had put it, toward my favorite orange fruit. "Okay, Dalton. In your professional opinion, what are pumpkin green-flags?"

He tipped his chin toward the seemingly endless rows.

"Sturdy stem, even color, no soft lumps. And a pumpkin should make you smile."

Smile. My mouth obeyed; my chest didn't. Last night ghosted in, reminding me of how Harrison had called me pumpkin, which elevated the tour to *Awkward: Deluxe Edition.* So, of course, I made a joke. "Ah, so we're judging gourds and ghouls by their dating profiles. Left swipe on limp stems. Right swipe on firm lumps."

That's PG-13, right?

Harrison's jaw ticked once. It was minuscule, but I had a PhD in Harrison Micro-Expressions and that one read, *keep it moving.*

Patch nosed a mini pumpkin; it popped free and pinballed between my boots. Dalton toe-stopped it like a soccer pro before it took me out, because, of course, it totally would have. Marty threw us a thumbs-up, which I interpreted to mean the hearts were scrolling like fairy dust on his screen. I could almost hear the chat: *Kiss him! Team Dalton! Team Chaos!*

Great. Fantastic. Exactly the circus my nervous system had ordered.

"Coordination," Dalton teased. "Another green flag."

"Guess that counts me out." I laughed nervously and pointed at the camera. "Right, spooky friends?" Bending to retrieve the baby pumpkin, I held it up for the live like I was one of those late-night TV salespeople. "This one is giving 'will support your goals and look cute in photos.'"

Off to my right, Harrison flashed two fingers: tighten. The gesture wasn't for the audience. It was for me. *Clip the flirt.* I breathed through my nose and kept my on-air voice sunny out of spite because one [incredibly hot] make-out sesh did not make Bossy McBossy-Pants my producer.

"Lightning round," I chirped as we made our way down the next row. "Carve or paint?"

"Carve first, paint later."

"Pumpkin spice latte or black cof—" My brain started mathing before my mouth finished talking because there was no better way to describe Harrison and me. I was seasonal and a little extra, while he was the straightforward and dependable everyday cup. A jingle played in my head: *The best part of waking up, is Fol—*

Marty windmilled, bringing me back. "Coffee," I blurted. "I meant black coffee." A nervous chortle escaped as I looked into the lens. "Live shows are my Roman Empire."

Dalton cut me a boyish grin. "Depends who I'm with."

I let out a performative gasp and tipped the camera a conspiratorial look. Harrison's hand slid into view for half a second—flat palm, wrap soon—before he yanked it back like it had betrayed him. His mouth went very, *very* straight, which translated to a warning for either me or Dalton. Inconclusive. (Also: *Hi, jealousy, I see you.*)

"Comments, discuss without violence," I said, steering us toward a pyramid of medium pumpkins that had me hoping the orchard had good liability insurance. I'd had a third question, but it had run straight into the corn, likely to never be heard from again. "We'll circle back," I told the viewers and myself.

Patch spotted a scarecrow and committed to friendship at full speed. Dalton lunged. I chased the leash. I windmilled, recovered, laughed like I wasn't one wobble away from becoming seasonal slapstick. The poor scarecrow never had a chance. Death by hay bale.

"Donuts for agility?" I panted into my mic. All of the

animal wrestling that morning had kickstarted my appetite. I would fail miserably as a farmer.

"Absolutely."

Patch, apparently already bored with his new friend, set his sights on me. Before I could meet a similar fate to the scarecrow's, Dalton grabbed my waist and whirled me out of the path of destruction. Patch continued on toward the pony pen.

Holding a hand to my chest, I thanked him, adding, "Shouldn't you go after him?"

"No need. He'll do the zoomies for a bit, then make his way toward the concession stand for a treat."

With the chaotic moment behind us, I became painfully aware of the fact that Dalton was holding me, so I cleared my throat and extricated myself. I probably shouldn't have looked toward the camera, but impulse control was not something I had a lot of. Marty held a fist over his mouth, suppressing a laugh. Beside him, Harrison stood ramrod straight with a darkness in his eyes that could kill a rhinoceros. His glare was locked on Dalton, like a lion who had his prey in sight.

It probably shouldn't have been such a turn on, but goodness, it took all I had to keep from launching myself at him right then and there. But I was a lady, and ladies don't launch. Besides, he had Winnie on his back, and I would not endanger her because of my libido.

Marty did his two minutes finger-whirl. Harrison mirrored it, smaller, tighter. His eyes skimmed from Dalton to me and stuck, the way a needle sticks in a groove. Not a smile. Not a frown. Just held. If I didn't know any better, I'd say his expression promised punishment of the bedroom variety. But this was *Harrison*. The man was wearing a

Where's Waldo? t-shirt under his cardigan for crying out loud. (Spoiler alert: Waldo was standing beside a popcorn machine over Harrison's lower-left ribcage.)

"Shaunie," a man's voice called over my shoulder. "Do you still want that donut?"

Pull it together. I smoothed my hands down the front of my sweater, immediately regretting it because the sensation made me *ick*. "Sorry. Yes."

"Cool. Thought I lost you for a sec."

I summoned a coy laugh, then focused on the camera. "We're going to indulge in some autumn treats, which I wish you could try because the smell is insane, but before we go, Dalton, give our friends at home one last pumpkiny hot tip."

"Don't overthink it," he replied—to me, not the camera.

"Or in my case, always overthink it." I clamped my hands together. "Dalton says pick the pumpkin that makes you smile, and I say—"

He leaned in. Polite, telegraphed. Like a gentleman offering an option and an out. Time elasticized. I turned at the last second, so his lips met my cheekbone. "Green-flag move," I said, letting the audience hear the smile in my voice. "Cheek only. We're a PG-13 pumpkin patch."

Dalton chuckled.

I refused to pay any attention to Harrison.

Taking a few steps toward the camera, I closed with, "Stay spooky, tip your farm staff, and send us your porch pics. Bye for now."

Marty sliced a hand, signaling we were clear, then pulled off his headphones, grinning. "Numbers were bonkers. Chat was unhinged. Ten out of ten."

"Great." My smile dropped off my face like a prop.

Harrison didn't move.

Dalton, reading the room like a pro, nudged my arm. "Rain check on donuts?"

"That would be good. I'm not feeling so well. I get these migraines that sneak in out of nowhere." I pressed my temples to sell the bit. It wasn't a total lie, because I was prone to those demonic headaches, I just didn't have one right that second.

"Can I get you anything?" His concerned tone was consistent with the *good guy* analysis I had made of him.

"No, thanks. I'm going to hole up in the dark and lie down."

"Okay, well, feel better."

"Thanks."

He gave me a gentle hug goodbye, then went off to find Patch. No doubt, Dalton would make a great husband. He was the kind of man I *should* want.

A cool breeze carrying the scent of cinnamon brushed my face, making the skin on my neck prickle. That's when it hit me: Esme's prophecy. I hurried toward Harrison who was already packing up gear.

"Hey, can we talk?" I asked.

"A little busy here."

"Yeah, I know, but—"

"Not now, Shaunie." He zipped up the bag and the sound echoed up my spine.

Because I apparently needed to confirm the obvious, I asked, "Are you okay?"

"Fine," Harrison replied, which is the least fine word in any language, as he picked up the bag. "I need air. I'm going to take a walk." There it was. The quiet retreat. The space he took when his feelings threatened to pour out of their neatly labeled cabinets.

"Okay," I said with careful intention, like disarming a bomb. "Do you want company?"

"No." His voice was as subtle as lit dynamite. "Not right now." He dropped the bag beside Marty. "Mind taking this?"

"You're not coming with?"

"I'll find my own way later." He turned without so much as a glance over his shoulder.

"Wait, Harrison."

"I said, not now." There was a severity in his conviction that stopped the bats in my gut mid-flight.

Sweat beaded on my forehead and an all-too-familiar weight planted itself on my chest. "Winnie," I croaked.

He stopped just as my jaw locked with tension. Wordlessly, he removed the backpack, placed it on the ground with a sense of care that gave me hope the ice around his heart would thaw eventually. Then, he left. Just...left, with the path swallowing his footsteps.

My breath caught—no, it was strangled in my throat by the invisible hand that had been there my whole life, reminding me that I wasn't worth staying for.

Winnie cried out, and my feet carried me to her. I fell to the ground, unzipped the bag, and brought her to my chest. She purred against my racing heart, coaxing it into a slower rhythm. I took an intentional breath. Then another.

Five things you can see. Balloon. Stroller. Wheelbarrow. Corn stalks. Pony.

Four things you can touch. Winnie's fur. The grass. My rings. Winnie's collar.

Three things you can hear.

I worked my way through all five senses, and by the time I'd completed the somatic exercise, I was calm enough to stand. Choosing to carry Winnie, I slung the empty back-pack over my arm.

Marty, mercifully oblivious or professionally pretend-ing, clapped my shoulder and offered me a water bottle. "Ready to head back?"

I nodded, took the drink, and followed him to the parking lot.

Back at the inn, Marty told me he would monitor socials for the rest of the day, so I didn't have to be online, which I greatly appreciated. Then he hurried upstairs to edit footage while I lingered in the lobby. Winnie had on her harness and was exploring every nook. Well, as far as the leash allowed. I imagined her sensing the stories behind each antique object because she was sensitive like that.

"Oh, good. I was hoping to run into you," Betty stepped out from behind the counter. "We have taken care of the issue with the pipes, so you or your partner can be moved into a new room tonight."

The thought of that stabbed me in the heart. Having separate rooms probably would've been the smart thing since Harrison and I were very much on a train ride to Whatever-Comes-After-Friends, even if we were presently in different cars. Me, with the luggage, buried under bags stuffed with feelings I could no longer ignore. Him, in the maintenance car, tightening bolts on anything that had shaken loose.

Winnie rubbed my calf, then circled through my legs, wrapping her leash around my ankle like she was trussing a roast. "Subtle, ma'am," I told her, doing a one-footed shimmy to unwind.

Betty's brows tipped up. "So, new room?"

"Thank you," I replied, meaning it, "but we're going to stay put."

Her gaze softened. "You're sure? We have a king on the second floor that's very quiet. No... ahem... plumbing surprises."

"The suite suits us," I said, because I turn to puns when I'm nervous. I wanted to be where he'd look first. If he came back and I wasn't there... Nope. I stood in my resolve, determined to see things through.

Betty studied me for half a beat, like she could read the footnotes in my brain. "All right then." She slid a small packet across the counter. "Extra tea for you because it's good for the soul. And these are for Miss Winnie." The label read *Salmon Stars* in cheerful handwriting.

Winnie pretended not to care because she was above begging, then tried to climb the counter.

"Thank you."

As if on cue, three soft taps sounded somewhere behind the check-in cubbies. Betty didn't flinch. She only lifted one corner of her mouth, the way people do when they've decided to call a thing what it is without writing it down.

"Pipes," she said mildly.

"Obvi," I agreed, even though I knew better, and tightened my grip on Winnie's leash. I took the stairs two at a time, as though getting to my destination faster would keep me from changing my mind. Staying put wasn't passive, it was a choice. And I was choosing to be exactly where he'd find me.

HARRISON DIDN'T RETURN to our room that afternoon. The clock downstairs chimed seven times, reminding me the outlook for that evening wasn't promising either.

Marty texted not long after to ask if I wanted to go to dinner.

Me: I already ate, but thanks.

I hadn't. My belly bats vetoed the thought of food with dramatic head shakes.

Me: Have you heard from Harrison?

Marty: No, why?

I stared at the glaringly empty chaise.

Me: No reason. Enjoy dinner.

Then, because honesty sometimes wins, I sent another:

Me: If he checks in, let me know.

Marty: Will do.

The radiator was quiet that night. No drumline behind the headboard. Just me, the cat, and a suite that didn't know what to do with my cloudy aura.

Nine passed. Then ten. The part of me that had learned to be cool, to be fine, to be chill in the face of silence tapped the glass like, *we've trained for this.* I knew how to wait for footsteps that wouldn't come, while holding onto hope that they would.

I filled the electric kettle with water and turned it on simply because it gave my hands a job. Winnie followed the cord like it owed her money, then flopped theatrically across my foot. "Emotional support loaf," I told her, and retrieved my tarot deck from my purse before dropping onto the bed.

I knocked on the stack three times, cut, and shuffled. Two jumpers tumbled into my lap:

The Hanged Man and *Queen of Cups*.

"Okay," I whispered. "Look at things from a new perspective. Trust my intuition. Trust the cosmos." That last one was tough.

I shuffled again and let gravity do the choosing. Cards slid down in a clumsy river:

The Tower. Brace for collapse.

The Sun. Rebirth and new beginnings.

Knight of Cups. Leading with heart in hand.

The Lovers. An aligned decision.

Steam squeaked from the kettle like it was also stressed. I poured it over the tea bag, added honey, and set the mug on the nightstand. Winnie decided the Knight was edible and tried to drag him under the bed. "Winifred," I warned, rescuing the card. "We lead with heart, not teeth."

I stared at the spread like it was a sentence I'd been avoiding. The *Queen of Cups* asked me to listen to my gut, which was whispering that timing and rejection were not the same thing. *The Hanged Man* asked for a pause without self-abandonment. *The Sun* promised the room wouldn't stay dark. And the *Knight?* A ridiculous, hopeful part of me read him as a man who'd find his words and bring them to my door. The Lovers didn't say *he's your destiny*, rather that I got to choose.

Esme had told me I'd understand the prophecy if I listened when the noise quieted. The suite was uncharacteristically silent, like someone had hit mute on a haunted house. I laughed once—soft, unbelieving, because, of course, the answer was to listen.

I reclined on the mattress and exhaled. My brain worked overtime to protect me from silence, but I'd spent a lifetime interpreting it: family dinners where "inside voice" had meant smaller, quieter; school nights where "you're exhausting" had been offered as a joke and had landed like a verdict. I had learned to apologize for existing loudly because it bought me another day at the table. When people didn't know what to do with me, I did it for them and disappeared first (often in plain sight).

I had been unlearning all of that in therapy. My therapist was on a ninety-nine–year lease she just didn't know it, because I liked who I was becoming, and she had played a big part in that build.

SO, yeah. Harrison's vanishing act pressed every bruise I pretended I didn't have. *The Tower* wasn't just fear of losing him. It was the crumble of a coping mechanism that had kept me safe, and lonely, in equal measure. Maybe the closet needed cleaning out to make space for something better. And there it was... The answer I'd been grasping for all week. Accessing it was as simple as going inward and listening to what my heart had known for far longer than I'd realized.

"I choose him," I said, very quietly, like a secret I'd finally told the right person.

Winnie chirped from the pillow and loafed against my thigh, purring like a tiny engine trying its best. I checked my phone for the millionth time. *Nothing.* I placed it facedown before I invented a new sport called Doom Scroll Marathon.

I turned off the lamp, sending the room into a soft darkness, the kind that pressed gently instead of swallowing whole. I closed my eyes and pretended I was a person who didn't count the seconds.

I was not.

Sometime after midnight, a floorboard creaked in the hall, then went still. Not ghostly. I held my breath and waited. *Nothing.* Just an old building remembering the weight of someone who wasn't there.

THIRTEEN

Wakefield Orchard looked different early in the morning before the crowds overtook its peace. The air smelled like damp hay, and the fields were fogged in a way I would've called romantic if my ribs hadn't welded themselves into a shield. I'd texted Dalton a little after seven that morning asking if I could come by to chat with him, sans cameras (and producers). I'd woken up to a chaise as empty as it'd been when I'd gone to bed, but sleep had solidified a lot of the clarity I'd gotten the night before, and I knew what I had to do.

Dalton was already there, leaning against a fence post, Patch sitting perfectly like he knew when a moment wasn't about him. The dog's tail thumped anyway because joy has no respect for tone. As a proactive attempt to avoid another incident, I'd left Winnie in the car, snuggled up in her carrier.

"Hey." He gave me a quick side hug, suggesting he knew why I was there.

I crossed one ankle over the other to keep from reorganizing the gravel. "Hey. Thanks for meeting me."

"Of course." He searched my face once, then didn't make me do the small talk. "What's up?"

I'd rehearsed a bit in the shower and during my drive over, but in that moment, my practice went to pieces. "I wanted to say this in person. This has been fun, but I can't keep..." I flicked my wrist. "Whatever this is. Moving forward."

He nodded, no flinch, just listening.

I fished around my memory for the words. "It's not something you did. You're great. You're a green-flag pumpkin with a sturdy stem." I grimaced because that had sounded better in my head.

"Hard to compete with my own metaphor," he said wryly.

"I'm sorry," I blurted, then corrected myself because—growth. "I'm not sorry for being honest. I'm sorry if it stings."

He nodded once. "It's not a surprise." His eyes held the type of kindness that made you want to be a better human. "I like you, Shaunie, but it always felt like I was more into it than you were."

"Valid. As much as I didn't want to admit it, the prophecy added pressure I couldn't get past." The morning chill was seeping in, so I tucked my hands into my jacket pockets. "I keep trying to want the safe option. The kind that makes sense on paper, and that my mother would approve of."

His mouth twitched as though he could relate.

"But that's not fair to either of us. I don't want to string you along while I sort out feelings..." I trailed off. "Yeah."

"So this is about Harrison," Dalton said. No edge, just verifying.

"Partially," I admitted. "But it's mostly about me not

pretending. I wanted to be honest before this became a story we both resent. I don't know how things will shake out with Harrison. I only know that, right now, I can't be available for more than friendship with anyone else."

Patch leaned his whole weight against my leg, then licked my knuckles like he was notarizing the statement. I huffed out a breath that wasn't quite a laugh.

"I figured. You don't look at me the way you look at him." He lifted a shoulder, easy. "You're great, Shaunie, but I'd rather be your friend than your placeholder."

"That's fair." I exhaled and saw my breath. "Sorry, again. I appreciate you not making this harder."

He shrugged like a decent human does when they choose not to be the villain in the story. "Thanks for not doing this on camera. That would've sucked." He cracked a smile, then sobered. "And you should never apologize for choosing what you actually want."

I nodded. "Working on that."

He offered a quick, contained hug that didn't linger. "Rain check on donuts," he said. "As friends."

"As friends," I agreed.

He whistled softly, and Patch trotted after him, stopping once to look back at me like he was checking that I was really okay. I lifted a hand in assurance.

I wasn't sure what waited for me with Harrison; I just knew the Dalton part was done, and it was the right kind of done.

MARTY HAD RESERVED Blackbird Books for our studio that morning. A sign on the door read, *Private Event. Ticketholders Only.* My conversation with Dalton had me running a bit behind schedule, so when I entered, the store was already buzzing with townspeople. Their chatter concealed my arrival, giving me the opportunity to scan the room for Harrison. It didn't take long to find him standing in the nook that was set as our stage. Two armchairs and a velvet loveseat curved around a low table with waters, tissues, and a printed *Please Silence Phones* card. In front of that were twenty-or-so mismatched chairs for the audience.

Harrison already had his headphones on, and he had changed his clothes, which meant he must've returned to our suite at some point that morning. As if my stare tugged a thread, he looked up. The air flickered hot, then cold, like someone had opened a freezer in my chest. Stealing my spine, I circled around the coffee cart, threaded through the crowd, and passed a row of carved pumpkins by the registers that were grinning like they were eagerly anticipating the tea we would spill.

"Morning," my co-host said, as I approached, neutral as a lab report.

"Morning," I returned, bright and normal, determined to pretend the night hadn't hollowed out a place between my lungs—at least until we finished taping.

"Way to make me sweat, Shaunie." Marty slid between us like Switzerland in a puffy vest.

"Sorry. I had something to take care of."

He hooked his thumbs through his belt loops. "Okay, team. Couples at ten past. We'll do three mini-interviews with Esme matches from different years. Keep it snappy, keep it sweet. Remember, even though we aren't broadcasting this live, we do have witnesses."

"Copy," Harrison said, eyes not leaving his phone screen.

"Copy," I echoed as I shed Winnie's carrier and stowed her off stage right.

Marty encouraged everyone to find their seats while I mic'd up and settled into my chair. I flipped through show notes on my iPad, pretending the bullet points were more interesting than the man lowering into the chair beside me.

Should I have held strong and kept to myself? Yes. Did I? Nope.

"I guess we're rolling right into this, huh?" I kept my eyes on the tablet because meeting his would've cracked me open.

"Guess so."

"We could've worked this out before, you know."

"Yeah," he said, even. "We could have."

That knocked me off balance for half a second. I looked up, ready to ask why he hadn't come back, but Marty chose that moment to point at me, wink, and clear to the side.

My personal life had to wait. Ever a professional, I slid on my host voice, like a jacket that almost fit. "Hey, spooky friends. Welcome to *The Unexplained Files*. I'm Shaunie, here with Harrison, at Blackbird Books in Sage Hollow, New Hampshire. We've been filming in this charming town all Halloween week, and I must say, the festivities truly do measure up to the hype. Joining us today is a spooktacular audience and a few special guests."

Following the script, Harrison took the next bit. "In a moment, we will be joined by three couples, paired together by local legend, Esme the Medium Matchmaker. If you caught our last episode, then you know Esme uses her abilities," his voice laced with skepticism on that word, "to hook people up with their soulmates."

"That's right, she does," I chimed in. "Single people travel from all over the globe for a chance at receiving a prophecy from Esme."

"Shaunie was the recipient of one this week," he blurted out, off script.

I'd been in the game long enough to build decent ad lib skills, but that threw me. It wasn't the time or place to reveal how that had turned out. I was saving that conversation to have in with Harrison in private. After clearing my throat, I replied, "Yes, I was." Vague was safe territory.

"Now you want to act shy about it? You've taken our listeners on your dates with Dalton the orchard guy all week." His laugh had an edge it didn't need. "Well, almost all of them."

"No, 'almost.' All of them. You were there, remember?"

Marty windmilled with his clipboard to direct us back on track.

I raised my brows to say I wasn't the one who'd gotten us *off* track. (First time for everything.) "Let's bring up our first couple before I file an HR complaint," I said through my plaster grin, receiving a few restrained chuckles.

"David and Minh, come join us."

The men came up the aisle, hand-in-hand. Marty clipped their lavs with nimble fingers and gave us the go signal.

"Welcome," I said, warmth dialed back to sincere. "How long have you two been together?"

"Eight years," David said, beaming at Minh. "Esme matched us at the Harvest Festival."

"Like you and Dalton," Harrison remarked, feigning enthusiasm.

"Harvest magic all around." I smiled at the audience instead of at him. "What did Esme tell you to look for back then? A sign? A vibe?"

David's fingers tightened around his husband's. "She

said, 'Find the person who makes the small things feel like big care.'"

Minh cleared his throat. "For me that was tea. I bring him a cup every morning before he wakes up. It's not profound."

"It absolutely counts," I said. "Eight years of morning tea is a love story."

Harrison finally glanced up. "Correlation isn't causation, but morning rituals correlate nicely with staying together."

I leaned in. "Do you remember the moment you knew the match was right? Was it the tea? A conversation? Something that clicked?"

David nodded. "I was in line at the festival for apple cider donuts. Minh was in front of me and got the last one."

Minh took over. "When I turned around, he looked disappointed, so I offered to share it with him."

My chest did a tiny thaw. "Small things, big care. I'd say that fits. Okay, before we let you off the hook. First fight after the match—what was it and what did you learn?"

"Paint colors." David laughed. "We learned to pick samples, not whole gallons."

"Data-driven compromise," Harrison murmured. "Endorsed."

We excused them and invited up the next couple. Before we resumed, Marty crouched between Harrison and me, and whispered, "Whatever is going on with you two, squash it."

I smushed my palms together and made a splat sound for extra effect.

Harrison, true to form, did nothing.

Marty cleared the stage.

I adjusted in my seat, lengthening my spine. "Please welcome Liz and Mark."

"How long?" I asked, already grinning at her round belly.

"Us, three years," Liz said before pointing to her stomach. "Him, twenty-seven weeks."

I offered congratulations, then asked about their prophecy.

"Esme told me, 'He returns the cart.' First day I met him, at the grocery store, he returned three. And that was before he even went in to shop."

"A good Samaritan," I complimented.

"Or baseline adulthood." Harrison deadpanned. "Encouraging either way."

The barb skimmed my skin and stuck. "We are pro-baseline adulthood on this show." The setup was too perfect to turn down. "Like facing your problems instead of running away and feeling your feelings instead of pretending they don't exist."

"And admitting what you want instead of going with what you think you should want." His mention of the bit from my prophecy I had revealed to him, and only him, had me spinning my rings to the point of them nearly taking flight.

"What surprised you most after being matched?" Harrison asked, moving on so seamlessly it irritated me.

Mark wore an uncomfortable expression, likely attributed to our bickering, but answered, "How natural it was. I almost let her go without asking for her number, but something in my gut told me to be brave. I went straight up to her and started a conversation. It felt like we'd always known each other."

"Well, we do endorse listening to your gut," I shot back,

too bright. "Sometimes the map knows before the driver does."

"All the time." Harrison clicked his pen.

"What?"

"Maps are fixed. Drivers are human. Maps know first."

"Spicy take from Mr. North Star." My smile dripped with sarcasm.

Marty coughed in an attempt to rein us in.

I read off my tablet, "Now, for our final couple, Maxine and Jonah."

Two college kids in thrifted sweaters shuffled up, mirroring shy smiles. Marty clipped their lavs and ghosted back behind the book cart.

I welcomed them. "How long have—"

"Maps aren't prophecies," Harrison interrupted, voice even, eyes still on the iPad. "Since we're all very into North Stars today."

I kept my smile aimed at the audience. "And since we're all very into basic adulthood, we could save the op-ed for after we let the couple speak."

"Not everything needs to be contrived content," he returned, still not looking at me.

I scoffed. "Wild take coming from a man who stayed out all night and showed up to work, still mad, and intent on airing it out."

Maxine's eyes darted to Marty like, *is this part of it?*

"I left to keep from saying something I didn't mean and couldn't undo." Harrison's jaw ticked. "And I wasn't mad when I was driving back to the suite this morning to apologize."

"You were—what?"

"I was coming to apologize," he repeated, finally looking

up. "And then I saw your car turn down Wakefield Road at eight-fifteen."

A collective inhale rolled through the audience like they'd been handed popcorn and then told not to chew.

I scrunched up my face. "Okay, and...?"

"The only destination on that road is the orchard."

"That's where Dalton is," I remarked, because stating the obvious was cheaper than screaming.

"Exactly."

"What's your point?" My grip on the iPad tightened.

"Tomorrow is Halloween, which, according to your precious prophecy, means today is your last chance for a 'kiss that will change everything,'" he mocked. "And you didn't have a date scheduled with him today, so..."

"So, what? You think I went there to kiss him?" The idea was so absurd it was laughable.

He shrugged. "I made a conclusion."

"More like, jumped to one. Vaulted, in fact."

"Guys," Marty stage-whispered from the side, clipboard windmilling. "Button this and regroup—"

"For the record," I said into the mic before my courage could flinch, "I went there to end it with Dalton. Kindly. Off-camera. That's why I was there."

Silence changed density. Somewhere near the coffee cart, a spoon clinked like it wanted to help.

Maxine half-raised a hand. "We can come back."

"I'm so sorry," I returned, mortified. "You've been wonderful. We're... malfunctioning."

Marty stepped in with his producer's smile that said, *gotta love show biz.* "Five-minute stretch," he announced to the room as if nothing catastrophic had occurred. "Help yourselves to coffee in the back."

Chairs scraped. Coats rustled.

Harrison set his tablet down like it weighed ten pounds. "We need to talk," he said, low, only for me. "Not here."

"Agreed."

Marty angled his head toward the staff hallway. "Break room is free." As if he sensed this would not be the quick fix he hoped it would, he added, "I'll get rid of everyone."

We stood. We didn't touch. We moved away from the little stage, I scooped up Winnie, and we slipped into the narrow hall behind him. The bookstore's noise softened behind us, and the quiet helped me breathe a little easier.

The break room was the size of a generous closet. A vending machine hummed in one corner and there was a *Label Your Lunch* sign on the fridge beside a small bistro table. Against the long wall was an overused loveseat I went straight for.

Harrison hovered by the table. "I'm sorry. I built the wrong story."

My throat unknotted a notch, and I unzipped Winnie's bag, letting her roam free. "You did."

He gripped the back of a chair. "Why did you end it with him?" It wasn't an accusation, rather an invitation.

"Because I finally listened." I crossed one leg over the other. "Last night, our room was so quiet. My brain was quiet, too. Well, relatively. Esme told me I'd understand the prophecy when the noise silenced, and I did."

He nodded, encouraging me to continue.

"I've been trying to want what's safe, what looks good on paper, what would make my mother say 'finally.' That's how I've kept myself... acceptable."

"Siobhan—"

"Let me finish." I held up my hand. "My whole life I shrank myself to fit into the molds my family, friends, teachers, bosses—you name it—wanted me in. I've done a lot of work to break out of those molds. Therapy, my vlog, even our podcast, have all helped with that. There are at least a quarter-million strangers in this world who like me, chaos and all."

He offered me a gentle grin.

"Dalton was me repeating an old pattern. Surrendering my growth to my nervous system's comfort zone, but I'm done abandoning myself simply to be picked," I said, the truth making my voice steadier. "Whether you were in the picture or not, I would've ended it."

His eyes went warmer than the room. "I'm proud of you."

"Thanks. Me, too."

Harrison gestured toward the cushion beside me. "May I?"

"Sure."

The springs compressed under his weight and, while we weren't touching, a zing filled the narrow gap between our thighs.

"I realized something else," I continued.

"What's that?"

"You're the only person who has ever truly seen me for me. You don't judge my quirks; you don't get frustrated when I lose focus, and trust me, I know it can be frustrating. Sometimes, you even anticipate my needs before I know I need them." My voice softened. "I've never had that before."

"You deserve that. You deserve more than that." He rubbed his palms over his jeans. "My mom was on the spectrum."

That one sentence made me hum with understanding.

"Routines were oxygen. Noise had to be managed, or the day fell apart." He tapped his ear. "She taught me earplugs for concerts, how to find the quiet sections in noisy stores, and that care can look like dimming a lamp without commentary."

Pieces clicked in my brain with embarrassingly loud relief. "That's why you're so good with me."

"Yeah. I guess." His throat cleared. "My mom was tuned to a higher frequency; I learned to tune with her. When she died, it was like a chord dropped out of the mix and the rest of the world kept playing. *They* were tuned differently, not her." He looked into my eyes and added, "Same with you. It's everyone else who's missing out on your brilliance."

My belly bats woke up at that.

Winnie purred like a jungle cat as she rubbed up against his legs. Without missing a beat, Harrison reached down to scratch her favorite spot between the ears. "We were all each other had. I never knew my father, and my mom's family had distanced themselves because they didn't understand her."

I felt that. Hard.

He stared at his lap. "I was lost for a long time after she died. Kind of still am."

Without thinking, I reached over and placed my hand on his. "We all get lost. I think the important thing is realizing you can always come home to yourself." That was what I had done when I'd been alone in that suite.

"You're right." He huffed. "Looks like I've been abandoning myself, too."

I gave his hand a squeeze.

"I never want to hurt like that again—the way I did after she passed. I decided the math was simple: you can't lose if you don't love, right? So, I built a life I can fix with a dial or a new cable."

The more he shared, the more it all made sense, and I thought of *The Hanged Man* tarot card. This information helped me see the whole situationship from a different perspective—his. "And then me," I whispered.

"And then you," he echoed, angling his body toward me best he could. "You charmed me from the first day I stepped onto your soundstage. I kept telling myself I could stand at a safe distance, but this trip has taught me that I can't. That I don't want to." He sandwiched my hand between his. "I am not proud of my behavior this week. The thought of losing you to another guy—and having to watch it from the front row—brought out a version of me I don't admire. He basically held up a mirror I couldn't ignore. Yesterday, watching you with him... after we had kissed."

The couch creaked.

Harrison sighed. "Siobhan, I fell for you somewhere between a test episode and a haunted elevator, it has just taken me this long to admit it because I've been pretending that staying still is the same thing as being careful."

I stared at the awful break room art (fruit in a bowl; why is it always fruit in a bowl?) so I wouldn't combust because I was pretty sure he'd just told me he loved me, and no man had ever said that to me before. Why my brain chose that moment to ruin with distraction, was beyond me. I took a few breaths to help me process as I repeated his words in my mind. Then I said, "Careful doesn't mean frozen, Harry."

"Noted."

Winnie jumped onto the armrest beside me and nudged my arm. "Subtle," I told her. I was getting there but needed a second.

"What is it?" he asked.

"Self-abandonment," I blurted as I took back my hand.

He cocked his head but waited patiently for me to elaborate.

"Boundaries," I added because he liked that word. "You leaving and not returning, not calling or texting, wasn't okay. And the version of me who abandons her needs to appease others, would let you get away with it because I can kind of understand now why you did it but still, not cool."

His lips rubbed together. "You're right."

I hadn't expected him to own it that easily. "Where did you go?"

"Hotel a few towns over. I needed the quiet to think clearly, too."

"Oh."

Winnie pawed at the couch, and I had to shoo her away before she did damage. A couple of feathers poked through the material, and one caught on my sleeve.

"I'm sorry for leaving and for not calling. Another one of my actions this week I'm not proud of. And I promise, I'll never do that to you again. Whether you're my friend or—"

"Wait, you just want to be my friend?"

"No, no," he corrected. "I definitely want to be more than that, but I wasn't sure if you did."

"Hold please." I went to the table and used a napkin and pen to scribble a note, then crossed back to the couch and, standing in front of him, handed it over.

He read it and chuckled, then took the pen, responded, and handed the napkin back.

Do you want to be my boyfriend? [*Circle one*]
Yes
No

Below my handwriting, he'd written:

*Option C) I want to be your consonance. Good on our own,
but better together.*

I couldn't contain my squeal.

"Is that a yes?" He placed a hand on each of my hips.

"Yes, yes, yes," I chanted, each getting louder.

He laughed. "Noise ceiling."

"I don't care." I cupped his face, bent down, and planted a quick kiss on his lips.

His fingers kneaded into me. "I have one more question."

"What?"

"Will you come with me to see Esme?"

That threw me. "Sure, but why?"

His expression grew serious. "I want to talk to my mom."

"Let's go right now." I grabbed his hands and pulled him to his feet before he could change his mind.

FOURTEEN

Winnie peered out from her carrier bubble like a suspicious astronaut when Esme emerged from behind a curtain. She had her curls pinned back in an old brass comb that looked like it had known many women and kept all their confidences. "There you are," she said, with a content smile. "Right on time."

"You knew we were coming?" Harrison asked, brow raised.

I patted his shoulder. *Baby steps.*

"My job is to know. Come." She gestured toward the reading room where we had first interviewed her the afternoon we'd arrived in town. That felt like so long ago. "Sit. I've already made tea."

We perched at her small round table. No dim lights or theatrics, just Esme being calm in a way that soothes. She set two mugs down—chamomile, vanilla, and lavender wafted from the steam. Esme turned her palms up between us. "Before we start, consent and parameters. I don't 'take over.' I listen. The language a spirit spoke here in the physical world does not matter. They use my mind and emotions, signs and symbols, and anything I have ever seen, felt, done, or experienced to communicate. If it feels wrong, you say stop. Okay?"

"Copy," Harrison said, shoulders squared like he was signing a waiver.

"Okay," I echoed. Under the table, I gave his bouncing knee a reassuring squeeze.

Esme breathed in once like she was tuning an instrument. "There's a woman standing very close to you," she told Harrison gently. "Maternal. Practical. Her love is orderly. She has a particular way of doing things."

"That tracks." Harrison's jaw ticked, and I sensed a lingering hesitation.

Esme closed her eyes, as though she were meditating or deep in thought. Silence stretched through the seconds until her lids fluttered open. "She's making me feel her passing. Her journey was long. Cancer. All over." Esme ran her hands over her arms. "Was it in her blood?"

He nodded.

"You cared for her, didn't you? Kept her home and out of the hospital as much as possible. She says you brushed her hair, and when it all fell out, you gave her scalp massages." She sniffed the air. "Coconut oil with rosemary."

Harrison flinched at the mention of the scent, though the tea smelled only of lavender.

I nudged the mug toward him and whispered, "For your nerves."

His hand cupped around it, but he didn't drink.

Esme's eyes softened. "She is a powerful soul. Says she has been using the simplest things on purpose so you could catalog them without fighting them."

"Catalog?" I asked. "You mean she has reached out?"

"Cinnamon at odd moments. Feathers where there

shouldn't be feathers. Three knocks—always three—never two, never four."

"We've had noises," I offered, unsure how much I should divulge.

"She's polite." Esme's attention tipped toward me. "And she likes your pockets."

My hand went instinctively to my front pocket, which had been empty that morning. A pewter angel wing poked at the fabric. "I didn't put that there."

"I know." Esme sipped. "She asked me to open the door for you two this week. Not the big door—those you opened yourselves. Little doors."

"The Honeymoon Suite," he said, not a question.

"I mentioned it to Betty when the west wing pipes needed attention," Esme said, totally casual about being a logistics fairy. "Your mom's idea."

Harrison stared at the table like it was a waveform he was trying to read. "If this is real, why now?"

"Because you asked," Esme said simply. "You don't have to say it out loud; asking lives in the body." She tilted her head, listening again. "She says she wants you to *have* 'big time.' She says, 'careful' has kept you safe, but you deserve more than safe."

I felt that in my sternum. "I... yeah."

Esme gave me a small nod like she'd heard me elsewhere. Then she looked at Harrison's empty hands. "She's very loud about one more thing: the cedar box."

He went still. "I didn't bring it."

"That's all right." Esme's mouth softened. "Open it tonight. It belongs to both of you."

"Both of us?" I asked because surely, I'd heard wrong. The woman didn't know me, and I'd only been dating her son for like a minute.

Esme's gaze settled on me. "She likes who he is with you."

Harrison draped his arm around the back of my chair. "She would've loved you."

"She does," Esme corrected. "Our loved ones never leave us; they simply cease to exist in their physical form."

We sat in the type of comfortable small quiet that followed a truth. Somewhere near the back wall there were three soft taps, spaced like a little triangle.

"Plumbing," I said automatically.

"Mom." Harrison's smile reached his eyes.

Esme set her palms flat, closing the channel as gently as she'd opened it. "That's all she wanted for now. Go be people. Eat something. Open the box when you're ready."

Harrison stood like the gravity had changed. "Thank you."

"Tell her thank you," I added, because I suddenly needed to.

"She heard you." Esme's forehead creased. "And if you see Betty, tell her the triangle knocks are not a maintenance issue."

Harrison and I laughed. He took my hand, and we left the Ever After Emporium with our compass set toward an old inn with a ghost problem.

IN THE SUITE, Harrison dug through his bag, then set the small cedar box on the desk, wafting a faint woodsy note into the air. I unzipped Winnie, who hopped out, did a perimeter check, and claimed the chaise like she'd signed the deed.

"Food before feelings?" I asked, because blood sugar

solved ninety percent of my crises. "Or feelings before food?"

He did the tiniest wince-smile. "Parallel process. We order; we open."

"Look at you, multitasking." I grabbed the room service menu like it was a game show prize. "Chicken soup for me and..." I glanced up.

"Same," he said. "And bread."

I called it in, then we hovered around the desk in a silence that wasn't empty.

"Ready?" I asked.

"No," he replied honestly. "Yes." He slid the latch. The lid gave with a small sigh, as though the air in the room recalibrated. Inside was a small USB drive. No note. No jewelry (that had been my guess). Just the ordinary thing that turned the air sacred.

Harrison picked it up, then put it down, then picked it up again. "I don't have—"

"You do," I said, already at his laptop, already plugging it in, because whatever he lacked in immediate courage, I had in chaotic momentum.

A folder bloomed: *For Harrison*. Inside were a handful of nested audio files.

1_Start_Here

2_Recipe_CinnamonToast

3_Stories

4_For_Your_Person.

My throat tightened. "She really labeled a file like a treasure map."

"Accurate metadata," he said faintly, which in Harrison, might as well be a sob.

After carrying the computer to the coffee table, we settled on the floor, and I clicked *1_Start_Here.*

FIFTEEN

A voice, saccharine and sticky, like the sap running through the maples outside our window, streamed through the computer's speakers, "Hi, sweetheart."

Harrison inhaled like he'd been underwater.

"If you're hearing this, it means you did the brave thing. I am so proud of you. You probably have a list somewhere titled 'Reasons Not to Open the Box.' Cross it out. You can make a new list called 'Living.'"

He put his hand over his mouth.

I slid mine to his knee and left it there. "She knew you well."

"I'm recording these on a good day," she continued, matter-of-factly. "I have more good days because people I love have made space for me to be myself. That's you, my boy. My angel. Harrison, you are my favorite person I ever met." Her laugh was playful. Infectious. I smiled.

My boyfriend's shoulders shook with a tearless cry.

I kissed his cheek, and whispered, "It's okay."

We listened to *2_Recipe_CinnamonToast*, which was exactly what it claimed to be, and also not. There were tips on toasting (low and slow), buttering (edge to edge), cinnamon-sugar ratio (scientifically generous), and the kind of instructions that aren't about food at all. "Eat it with someone who loves you as much as I do."

I nudged him. "We are *definitely* making that."

"Indubitably."

Room service knocked. *One—two—three.* Of course it did.

"Pipes," Harrison said, voice rough, as he went to get the tray.

We ate soup on the bed like teenagers while Winnie patrolled for contraband noodles.

3_*Stories* was a patchwork quilt of small memories. The sort of tiny moments you only kept if you were paying attention.

A Fourth of July parade when six-year-old Harrison had tugged her to the quiet curb and counted the way she liked, "one-two-three-pause."

The night he had labeled the drawers with blue tape so mornings wouldn't snag: *MUGS, COFFEE, SPOONS.*

His gentle three knocks on the bathroom door because anything else had startled her.

How when he'd been in high school, he had turned the city into a mix for her so noise became music: bus equals bass, crosswalk beep equals hi-hat.

The kitchen timer he'd set for her breaks while he'd sat on the hallway floor, narrating softly where he'd be when it rang.

By the end, Harrison had to use the pad of his thumb to wipe my tears. "What's wrong, pumpkin?"

"I can't believe you did all that for her."

"Why not? She was my mom."

"No one did those things for me." My voice cracked.

He brushed my hair behind my ear and pressed his lips to my temple. "I will."

I slid my arm around his back and pulled myself closer.

"Ready for the next one?" he asked.

"No." I finished the last bite of my broth-soaked bread.

"Later?" he asked, a hint of relief.

"Later."

He carried our empty dishes into the hall, then stowed his laptop on the desk before returning to the bed. "Now what?"

"Whatever we want. Perk of being an adult."

He laid on his back with his stretched above the pillows—an invitation. "Come here."

I rolled onto his chest, and his arm closed around my back. The consistent rhythm of his heartbeat brought my system to neutral. Sturdy. Comfortable.

Children's laughter carried on the breeze outside, a reminder that Halloween was on the horizon.

"Did you bring a costume?" I asked, although I knew what his answer would be.

"I don't wear costumes."

"But, Harry," I groaned. "Halloween is the most fun day of the entire year. Every morsel of autumn goodness culminates in this one holiday. There's nothing better."

He stroked my hair. "You ever think about why you love fall so much?"

"Three words: Pumpkin Spice Latte."

I felt the eye roll in his laugh. "No. It's science."

This ought to be good. "Enlighten me, wise one."

"Serious. My mom taught me this."

My ears perked up. "I'm listening."

"Think about it. Warm spices, hot fireplaces, cozy blankets, shorter days and longer nights."

"Check, check, check, and check."

"All things inherently comfortable. The focus is on rest."

I hummed in agreement while drawing lazy circles on his abdomen with my fingernail.

"For people like my mom—"

"And me."

"And you, autumn is that chance to slow down, go inward, limit overstimulation."

Without taking my head off his chest, I glanced toward his face. "That actually makes a lot of sense."

"Science."

"You know what else I learned recently is science?"

"What?"

My fingers dipped toward his waistband, and he sucked in a breath. "Attraction."

"Oh?"

"Ohhhh," I teased. "It's chemistry, Harry."

"Is it now?"

"Sure is." I worked on his belt buckle. "My chemicals, *really* like your chemicals."

"Do they?"

I hummed in agreement while unfastening his jeans. His checkered boxer shorts appeared behind the open zipper. In a so-not-sexy, but so-totally-me move, I hopped to my knees and crawled around to the foot of the bed.

"Where you going?"

I responded by grabbing his ankles and pushing them apart so I could fit between, then proceeded to prowl up between his legs until I ran out of runway.

He let out a reserved laugh. "You're adorable."

Gripping the hem of his tee—*Superman*—I eased it up,

revealing a set of abs I hadn't known were there. Six of them! "Harry," I exclaimed.

He gave me a knowing grin. "Yes, Siobhan?"

"You have muscles. Real ones." Unable to help myself, I flattened my hand over the bumpy terrain and rubbed, too fast to be sensual, but the perfect speed to satisfy my curiosity. "Have these always been here?"

At that, his laughter bubbled from his diaphragm. "Pretty much."

My gaze trailed to his. "And you hide them underneath a shirt? That's a crime, I'll have you know."

"Is it?"

"Yes. And I must insist you bring your EMF to every paranormal investigation from here on out."

"EMF?" He raised a brow.

"Extremely Muscly Frequency-O-Meter," I replied, like, *duh.*

He held up a hand. "My mistake."

Satisfied, I continued to roam over his torso, which was bare save for a narrow cluster of dark curls mid-chest. "Any other surprises you've been hiding?" I asked before tracing his nipple with my tongue.

He breathed out—a call for more.

I obliged.

"My pants," he whispered.

"I know you have a penis, Harry. I wouldn't call that a surprise."

He shook his head and his eyes sparkled with mischief. "Not what I meant."

My mind turned over a list of possibilities. "Do you have a Jacob's Ladder?"

He winced. "No."

I sat back on my calves. "A birthmark in the shape of a maple leaf on your hip."

"No."

"Butt?"

"Yes, pumpkin, I have a butt."

"No, the birthmark."

He shook his head.

"A scar down your thigh from wrestling alligators?"

Harrison rolled his eyes. "When have I ever mentioned alligator wrestling?"

"You never mentioned your abs either." I gestured toward the offending muscles. "Yet, there they are."

"Fine. No, to alligator wrestling. Statistically improbable."

"How come?"

"Boston's alligator population is a little light at the moment."

"Because you wrestled them all out of the harbor?"

He pinned me with a stare that said, *give it up*.

I tried not to appear too disappointed because that would've been cool. "If not gators, then sharks? We have those in Massachusetts."

"Stop guessing."

"Then how will I know what secret you're hiding in your pants?"

He slapped a palm to his forehead.

"Oh." It hit me. "I'll just check."

"Great idea."

"I can be pretty smart," I bragged as I went to war with his jeans.

Tugging.

Tugging.

Tugging.

I stopped at his ankles and gasped. "You have got to be kidding me," I squealed. "Hold on. No." I licked my thumb, touched it to his thigh and rubbed, then repeated the process for his other thigh.

"Good luck," he jested.

I rubbed my eyes. "You have full-leg tattoo sleeves? On both legs?" I bent forward to get a closer look. The man's legs were an homage to every cartoon tee I'd ever seen him wear. "Harrison." I put my hands on my hips. "You know what this means, right?"

"That I have tattoos?" he replied in earnest.

"No. This means you are a total sneaky-hot nerd," I exclaimed, trying to make my point land.

"A what?" His expression was giving perplexed, at best, mortified at worst.

"Only the best kind of nerd there is." I plopped down beside him, propping myself up on my elbow. "If I didn't know you and you walked into a room, I'd clock you as 'competent tech guy.' Fifteen minutes and a scandalized copy machine later, I'd be texting my group chat, *Help, the competent tech guy is devastating.* That's sneaky hot."

His face flushed red.

Because my filter did not know when to stop, I continued, "I'll put it in your terms. Species: Nerdus stealthicus. Habitat: near outlets. Diet: black coffee. Mating call: 'statistically accurate.' Identifiers: cartoon tees, perfectly lined up writing utensils, and leg tattoos you only notice when it's already too late for your dignity."

Still no response.

"You fix the hum in my audio, and the hum in my bod—"

He grabbed my face and kissed the words out of me. Our tongues twirled, picking up right where we'd left off the last time. Harrison excised me from my crew neck sweatshirt, then went straight for my pants, seemingly eager to get me on the same level of naked as him. I wholly approved of that gesture. This time, when he tossed my bra, three crystals tumbled to the mattress: one for luck, one for balance, and one for love.

When he rolled to kick his pants the rest of the way off, I seized the opportunity and climbed him with the shamelessness of a cat who knew she was desired, and he caught me with the steadiness of someone who'd spent a lifetime managing variables.

"I know we're supposed to do foreplay," I said as I straddled his hips, leaving nothing between us but his boxers and my panties.

He put a finger to my lips. "There's no such thing as 'supposed to' when it comes to sex."

Had I found the one activity Harrison didn't plan out minute-by-minute? Why, yes. I had.

Lifting his hips, taking me with him, he slid off his underwear, freeing himself from the cotton prison. Without giving me a moment to admire him fully nude, he slid my panties to the side and positioned himself at my entrance. Just as he was about to penetrate me, he groaned and halted. "Condom," he hissed.

"I have the patch."

His face twisted with uncertainty.

"Statistically speaking, Harry, condoms are only, like, eighty-five percent effective, whereas the patch is ninety-nine percent—"

He thrust inside me. "It's hot when you talk statistics."

"Is it?"

Nodding, he dug his fingers into my hips and lowered me until he was fully seated.

"Wow," was all I could manage. Movement wasn't necessary; simply being full of him satisfied this deep ache I had for belonging.

He rolled until we'd switched, and he was on top. My ankles locked behind his back and gripped the back of his head, because his hair was totally made for grabbing. We moved together; it wasn't swoony music or fireworks so much as consonance—frequencies layering until the room felt exactly right.

His forehead lowered to mine. "I could get used to this."

"Me, too," I whispered from the part of me that craved familiarity.

He quickened his pace. The ridge of his crown nudged the spot on my upper wall that made my toes curl.

"Just like that," I pleaded, biting his shoulder to muffle my cries.

His breaths grew staccato, and my soul sensed his body was close. I tilted my hips slightly, putting him precisely where I needed him to be.

"Oh, God," I mumbled into his shoulder.

"Shaunie, I'm close," he panted.

"Me, too."

Two more pumps and I was catapulted into the ether. Confetti cannons exploded in my entire body as I let myself feel every tingle—every spasm.

Harrison grunted and his pace halted, drenching me with his come, and I refused to let him go until he had given me every drop. Once I was satisfied that he had, he dropped to the mattress and rolled onto his back. "Cuddle," he called as he tried to catch his breath.

Happy to oblige, I snuggled into his nook.

.   .   .

AN HOUR LATER, we woke up in the same position, still naked, still cuddled. It had been the best nap of my life.

Harrison kissed my forehead. "I love you," he whispered, so low I almost didn't hear it.

"Really?"

"Yes."

"Even though it means you could get hurt?" Should I have asked that? Probably not, but the overthinking side of my brain never would've let it go.

"That's the measurable factor of my love for you. It is because I know I could be hurt, I can confidently assert I love you."

"I won't hurt you, Harry." I traced a circle on his chest.

He squeezed me tight. "I trust you."

"Good. But also, because I love you, too." Saying those words to him made all my belly bats cheer.

"You do?"

"Obvi." I swatted his stomach. "How could I not? My sneaky-hot, Knight of Cups."

"Now what am I?"

I giggled. "I have so much to teach you."

Our phones dinged at the same time, which could only mean one thing: Marty.

"Not now," I groaned. "Let's ignore—"

My phone rang with my producer's ringtone. I tossed my arm over my eyes with dramatic flare. "I simply refuse."

Harrison's phone rang next. "You know if we don't respond, he'll come up here."

I bolted upright. "But I'm naked."

"I will handle it." He grabbed his phone off the nightstand and answered, while I wrapped myself in a sheet as though Marty could see me through the phone. "Hello?" Harrison's tone was dry, as per usual. He hummed several times, then said, "Yes, I will tell her, but then we require being left alone for the remainder of the evening." His face gave nothing away. Another hum. "Good night." He tossed the phone aside.

Curiosity immediately got the best of me. "Tell me what?"

He scooted against the headboard. "News of our semi-public discussion today has made it to the internet."

I let out a sigh. "Yeah, well, we knew it would eventually."

"How do you want to handle this?" he asked.

"How do *you* want to handle this?"

"Asking you is a formality. I plan on letting the world know you're mine."

I lunged at him and gave him the biggest hug. "I like that plan."

"Good. Now, I'm going to shower, and while I do that, you have homework." He gestured toward his laptop. "There's a message waiting for you."

"But don't you want to hear it, too?"

"Later. She recorded it for you."

His lips grazed mine before he stood, and crossed to the bathroom, while I enjoyed watching him walk away.

Winnie picked her head up from what had become her spot on the chaise as I went to the desk and queued up the recording. I pressed play as I sank into the chair, gathering the excess sheet around my feet.

"Hello, future person," Harrison's mom said, and I couldn't help it; I laughed and pressed my fist to my mouth.

"Hi," I whispered to the screen like an idiot.

"I don't know your name."

"Siobhan," I replied, since I'd already committed to talking to a recording from nearly a decade ago.

She went on, "But if you're listening, you've already done something brave. You've made room for my son to be soft. Thank you. He will pretend he doesn't need that. He does.

He'll forget."

I swallowed hard.

"When he does, try this: don't argue him out of the shell. Put a cup of something warm in his hand and sit on the same side of the problem. He likes side-by-side."

My fingers reached for a pen, then stopped. It was a file. I could replay her forever, but I still wanted to write her down.

"A few notes, since I won't be in the kitchen pretending not to watch you both:

"First—he does better when something small is finished. If he looks far away, give him a corner to complete. He comes back faster when his hands remember he is useful.

"Second—he is stubborn about carrying things, so you don't have to. That is not always noble. Sometimes it's just heavy. Trade with him. Take the grocery bag. Let him put his head on your shoulder every once in a while. No medal is issued for holding it all. That goes for you, too.

"Third—he will bring extra batteries, extra socks, extra plans. Let him. He loves in redundancies. You don't have to need the spare flashlight for it to matter that he packed it."

The picture she painted began taking shape as the Harrison I had grown to know, and I smiled.

"He says he doesn't dance. He does at the sink, when he thinks you can't see. He will deny this. Don't make him prove it. Just enjoy the way his shoulders forget to be careful when there's soap and a song."

"Oh, Winnie, we will most definitely be testing that one."

"When he's proud of something, he gets quiet. It looks the same as doubt from far away. Learn the difference. Ask, 'Is this the proud kind of quiet or the worry kind?' He'll tell you if you give him the two choices."

I had a suspicion that one would come in handy, so I tried to commit it to memory.

"He will be late to say when he is hurt, because he wants the story to come with a solution. You don't have to wait. You can be the place a mess is allowed to land. Put a hand at the back of his neck and leave it there. That's the only instruction for that one."

Accurate. I nodded as though she could see me.

"He will study you. Not in the way people say, not to judge. He will learn where you set your cup and which sweater means you're tired. Let him. It will feel like standing in a patch of sun."

Also, accurate. A pale feather drifted down from who-knew-where and landed on the laptop frame, light as breath. I didn't move.

"A thing you should know is that he is loyal past the line of fashionable. If he chooses you, he will keep choosing you when it's raining, when it's late, when the thing you planned becomes the thing you survived. Please do not take advantage. Please also do not be afraid of it. You can lean.

"On the days the world is loud, don't make yourself smaller to match his quiet. Bring your whole self and see what happens. He is stronger than his hush.

"If you are sitting at a table together and something makes you both laugh at the same second, stop and notice it. That is the good life. People waste years looking for something louder.

"I worried, before I got sick, that I was the only person who knew how to read him. That is a terrible thing to realize—that you've put your whole heart in a single basket. If you are listening, it means I was wrong. I am very glad to be wrong."

My hand covered my heart of its own accord.

"I won't be in your way. I don't intend to haunt your light fixtures or knock pictures off your walls. I just wanted a way to wave."

I couldn't help but laugh at that as I picked the feather up off the keyboard.

"I don't know your name," she repeated, softer, "but I am grateful for you. I wanted the next person who loves him to have what I didn't—someone to say, 'Here are the cliff notes to my favorite human.' I hope you write your own pages on top of mine."

"You can turn this off now. Go find him and make something ordinary together. Ordinary lasts."

The audio clicked gently into silence, and the room felt bigger in the way rooms do when someone leaves them better than they found them.

I sat there a long second with my hand over my mouth because there wasn't a good place to put it. The bathroom door opened—quiet, careful. Harrison stepped in like he wasn't sure if the air would hold.

I turned the laptop so he could see the paused waveform and held up the feather.

He blinked hard and crossed the room in two strides. He didn't speak. He didn't need to. He sat beside me—side-by-side—and we let the ordinary start.

The radiator didn't so much as clear its throat.

EPILOGUE

The Sage Hollow Inn had turned its old ballroom into a low-key theater. There were rows of chairs, a tiny riser with two mics, and enough twinkle lights to moonlight as a constellation. A paper banner read, *The Unexplained Files: Halloween Live* in Marty's blocky Sharpie. In October, Sage Hollow didn't just lean into spooky, it lived up to the title of Unofficial Halloween capital of America. *Fight me.*

I checked my mic while Harrison adjusted something at the mixer. He clipped my lav to the strap of my khaki jumpsuit, fingers steady. His name patch read *MORETTI*. Mine read *SHAUNIE*, (yes, my doing) because subtlety is a costume, too. Winnie blinked at us from a chair near the hearth wearing a tiny white "ghost" cape with ear cutouts and absolutely no shame.

"Levels are clean," Harrison said. "You good?"

"Boo-tiful," I whispered, because restraint is not my brand.

Marty raised three fingers. The audience, locals and tourist in capes and flannels, settled. Betty dimmed the sconces. Somewhere in the wainscoting the was a *knock,*

knock, knock. A few heads turned. Betty didn't. Harrison and I exchanged knowing grins.

Marty counted us down. *Three. Two. One.*

"Hey, spooky friends!" I sang into the mic, and the room answered with cheers. "We are live from the Sage Hollow Inn on the best night of the year. I'm Shaunie, that's Harrison—"

He gave the room a quick nod that somehow counted as a smile.

"—and yes, Winnie is haunting us from the VIP row."

A small child in a pumpkin suit waved at her. She blinked back, magnanimous.

"WE'VE GOT STORIES, we've got candy, and we've got a very special guest," I continued. "Please welcome the Medium Matchmaker herself—Esme."

Esme slipped onto the loveseat in a dress printed with a crescent moon. She smelled like tea and something sweet I couldn't place. The applause held an affection I felt in my chest. "Esme," I said, "last year we learned a lot about listening. Tonight, we're hoping for the director's cut."

Esme's eyes twinkled. "Director's cuts are only for people who stay through the credits." She looked out at the crowd, then back at us. "Hello, loves."

We did a handful of fun ones: best ghost etiquette, worst corn maze, the ethics of stealing from your kid's candy haul. Harrison delivered one-liners like evidence, drier than the hayride, which was funnier because he didn't try. Our edges fit better than they ever had. Our timing had been practicing all year.

Then I shifted. "Okay, one serious one," I said, glancing

to Esme. "People ask us all the time, how do you know when it's the thing you keep?"

Esme's gaze softened, and the ballroom air seemed to hush so even it could hear. "You notice the small things that become big because they repeat," she offered. "A hand that finds your back without hunting for it. A laugh that makes your shoulders drop. A quiet that isn't empty." She tilted her head, listening to whatever station only she gets. "And tonight," she added, gentle as a secret, "I am shown a circle. Bright. A promise."

The audience did that collective inhale people do when life tries to outdo television. My heartbeat counted up like a drum fill. I looked at Harrison.

HE TOOK off his headphones and set them down carefully, like he was clocking out of one job to do another. No speech sat on his tongue; I could tell. He stood because his body knew before his brain did.

"Hi," he said into the mic, which was ridiculous and perfect. "I'm not good at... theatrical." The room laughed kindly. He looked at me, not the crowd. "I asked Esme to help with something tonight. I didn't want to make this about surprise because I wanted it to be about truth."

Heat dotted my cheeks.

He reached into his pocket and placed a small cedar box on the table between our mics. The familiarity made my breath stutter.

"To all of you, she's Shaunie: ghost hunter extraordinaire, who really owns her reputation as chaos wrapped in pumpkin spice."

The audience shared a knowing laughter.

"But to me, she's Siobhan," he said, precise and

somehow wrecked. "You are the woman who turned my life upside down, inside out, and statistically speaking, all around better. Will you marry me?"

He opened the box. A simple ring caught the light like it's sole job was to sit there and look pretty.

I stood so fast my chair skated. "Yes," I declared, too loud for the audio and exactly right for the night. My hands shook. My whole face grinned. "Yes."

The ballroom bloomed with applause and laughter. A pale feather drifted down and lodged itself in the twinkle lights above us, because of course, the Universe has a sense of humor.

Harrison rounded the table. He didn't kneel; it didn't feel like him. He stood, close enough that I could smell the faint soap on his collar and slid the ring onto my finger with careful hands I'd come to know as well as my own.

"Hi, fiancé," I whispered. Oh, who am I kidding? I shouted it so loud the shingles shook.

His mouth quirked. "Hi."

"Okay," Marty stage-whispered near the mixer, clawing us back to our jobs, "for the audio... kiss?"

"Rational," Harrison said, and the room laughed as I grabbed his jumpsuit and took the producer's note.

When we remembered we were still making a show, I turned to the crowd with a face I couldn't control. "Spooky friends," I said, voice wobbling. "I guess this just became a *very* special episode."

Esme pressed a hand to her heart. A ring is only a circle," she said simply. "The life is what you fill it with. Choose each other on the noisy days and the quiet ones."

We closed like we always do, side-by-side at the table with my hand on his knee and Winnie snoring like an air leak nearby.

"Stay curious," I said.

"Stay kind," Harrison added.

"And," we chimed, because some habits are worth keeping, "stay spooky."

The light on the recorder went dark. The room turned human again with people lining up to hug and hand us cookies and tell us which weekends in June were "obviously better for weather." A little angel with a paper halo tugged my sleeve.

"You dropped this," she said solemnly, offering the halo.

I hadn't, but I'd learned to stop questioning things in that town. "Thank you." I set it, crooked and perfect, on Harrison's curls. He didn't remove it.

Betty passed by with a tray of cider. "We kept the Honeymoon Suite ready," she whispered, like it was a punchline and a blessing.

Harrison laced our fingers and lifted them, not so the crowd could see, but so I could. He leaned close enough that I felt the word more than heard it.

"Home," he said.

"Home," I echoed.

And in a room full of people dressed as other things, we stood there exactly as ourselves—two nerds in jumpsuits, a cat in a sheet, and a promise bright enough to light up a town on Halloween.

NEXT STEPS

Want a FREE BOOK?
Get *Rescuing Griffin*
www.kayekennedy.com/rbc-prequel

Help others fall in love with Shaunie & Harrison by leaving
a review on Amazon, BookBub, and GoodReads.

Want more Small-Town Holiday Romance?

MERRY EX-MAS

A Second Chance, Small-Town, Christmas Romance

When a burnt-out attorney flees the city for a surprise
Christmas in her snowy hometown of Evergreen Falls, the
last thing she expects is to crash her car—or be rescued by
the ex she never got over. Snowed in together at a remote
inn with one room left and no cell service, old sparks

reignite amid the storm. But when the snow melts, will their rekindled feelings survive the thaw?
Gilmore Girls meets _Hart of Dixie_ in this heartwarming holiday romance between a small-town single dad and a curvy big-city lawyer.

You can interact with Kaye, chat all things romance, and get access to freebies in her exclusive **Facebook Group**: **Romance Reads that Kiss & Tell**

Join Kaye's Romance Readers Club and be the first to find out about new releases and giveaways! You'll also get free bonus scenes and fun extras.
Sign up at www.kayekennedy.com

ACKNOWLEDGMENTS

Without the following individuals, this story may never have been told:

• My fairy godmothers, for being the first safe space I've ever known; for encouraging me to keep pushing for higher goals; and for loving me back to life

• Mike, for your unwavering support and encouragement; for helping me learn how to live again; and for restoring my faith in happily ever afters

• Maria: One year ago, I was a shell, and you saved my life. I will never be able to express my gratitude enough. I love you, soul sister!

• My grandmother for fostering my love of reading from a young age and for always being my number one fan—no matter what I do.

• Pamela: Consider this me putting you on notice of the ninety-nine-year lease I have for your services! Like, Shaunie and her therapist, I would not be who I am today without you.

• Margot Miller, for coaching me into my unapologetic success era. You've inspired a lot of Shaunie's journey as she learned to step into her authentic self and live out loud.

• Jaycee DeLorenzo, for bringing my vision for the cover to life.

• Zelda, for editing my chaos monster.

• My KATs (members of my Facebook Group) for your loyalty, understanding, kind words, and support.

• YOU for taking a chance on love with my characters.

<u>Small Town Holidays Series</u>

If you loved Pumpkin Spice & Holidays, then this is your series! Feel-Good Standalone stories set in small towns during the holiday seasons

Merry Ex-Mas – Laurel & Jake

<u>Burning for the Bravest Series</u>

If you like alpha males with soft centers who love hard and make love harder, then this series featuring New York City firefighters is for you!

Burning for More – Dylan & Autumn

Burning for This – Jesse & Lana

Burning for Her – Ryan & Zoe

Burning for Fate – Jace & Britt

Burning for You – Kyle & Allie

Burning for You: The Wedding – Kyle & Allie

Burning for Love – Declan & Gwen

Burning for Trouble – Mack & Tori

Burning for Secrets - Brix & Georgia

Burning for Reality - Theo & Kenzie

Burning for Christmas - Keith & Brielle

Standalone set in the same world

<u>Flirting with the Finest Series</u>

Follow the men and women of the Special Investigations Task Force in New York City as they fight crime and fall in love.

Flirting with Forever – Hunter & Lauren

Flirting with Fame - Tai & Bellamy

Flirting with Faith - Erik & Aubrey

Flirting with Freedom - Cooper & Leila

<u>Rescued by the Rangers Series</u>

Follow a team of former Army Rangers turned independent contractors who've taken on the most challenging missions, but have struggled to find love. Until now.

Rescuing Griffin - Prequel to Book 1

Rescued by Chance – Griffin & Holly

Rescued by Loyalty — Nick & Mia

ABOUT THE AUTHOR

Kaye Kennedy is the author of contemporary romance and romantic suspense novels featuring everyday heroes who love hard and make love harder. Fun fact: she used to be a firefighter and now she writes about them! If you like steamy and soulful reads that will break your heart and put it back together again, then her stories are for you. In her books, you can always expect a happily ever after that kisses and tells.

She earned her degree in English Literature and taught college composition & literature classes before switching gears entirely and becoming an entrepreneur, starting multiple businesses. In addition to writing, Kaye sees clients as a psychic medium and serves as a coach for authors wanting to level up their careers.

While originally from New York, Kaye has lived in New Hampshire and Florida, but now calls Connecticut home. She is battling an invisible illness and resides with her rescue mutt turned service dog, Zeus, who is a character in Burning for Secrets. Kaye's real-life HEA is her favorite trope: friends-to-lovers (and will one day be turned into a book). When she isn't writing, she's out paddling on the water, indulging in a beach read, checking out a brewery, or feeding her wanderlust.

You can interact with Kaye and get access to freebies in her exclusive Facebook Group: Romance Reads that Kiss & Tell. If you really want to be entertained, check her out on TikTok @authorkayekennedy.